ODDS AGAINST SURVIVAL

The stakes were high—the outcome of the entire war.

That meant the game was worth it—no matter how high the risks.

Scott Gideon had to play the part of a German-speaking scientist—and bluff his way into the nerve center of the monstrous Nazi death factory.

His aide, the Dutch Jew, Joel In'Hout, had to play the part of an Arab on a camel-back journey through a land ruled by murderous native tribes.

And after that, the entire Phoenix team had to play their parts in action against the cream of the S.S. and the Luftwaffe in a battle that would be Phoenix's supreme challenge—and perhaps its last. . . .

TARGET: SAHARA

Exciting Fiction from SIGNET

                                                                        (0451)

- [ ] **HOUR OF THE CLOWN** by Amos Aricha. (097173—$2.95)*
- [ ] **PHOENIX** by Amos Aricha. (098455—$2.95)
- [ ] **EYE OF THE MIND** by Lynn Biederstadt. (117360—$3.50)*
- [ ] **GAMES OF CHANCE** by Peter Delacorte. (115104—$2.95)*
- [ ] **DOUBLE CROSS** by Michael Barak. (115473—$2.95)*
- [ ] **POSITION OF ULTIMATE TRUST** by William Beechcroft. (115511—$2.50)*
- [ ] **SAVANNAH BLUE** by William Harrison. (114558—$2.75)*
- [ ] **THE SEA GUERILLAS** by Dean W. Ballenger. (114132—$1.95)*
- [ ] **THE DELTA DECISION** by Wilbur Smith. (113357—$3.50)
- [ ] **HUNGRY AS THE SEA** by Wilbur Smith. (122186—$3.95)
- [ ] **THE LONG WALK** by Richard Bachman. (087542—$1.95)
- [ ] **THE RUNNING MAN** by Richard Bachman. (115082—$2.50)*
- [ ] **NIGHT AND FOG** (Resistance #1) by Gregory St. Germain. (118278—$2.50)*
- [ ] **MAGYAR MASSACRE** (Resistance #2) by Gregory St. Germain. (118286—$2.50)*
- [x] **SHADOWS OF DEATH** (Resistance #3) by Gregory St. Germain. (119991—$2.50)*
- [x] **ROAD OF IRON** (Resistance #4) by Gregory St. Germain. (122313—$2.50)*

*Prices slightly higher in Canada

Buy them at your local bookstore or use this convenient coupon for ordering.
THE NEW AMERICAN LIBRARY, INC.,
P.O. Box 999, Bergenfield, New Jersey 07621
Please send me the books I have checked above. I am enclosing $ _5—_
(please add $1.00 to this order to cover postage and handling). Send check or money order—no cash or C.O.D.'s. Prices and numbers are subject to change without notice.
Name _Ax3 B.A. EdwARDS_
Address _Box 334_
City _F.P.O NEw YoRk_ State _NEw YoRk_ Zip Code _09523_
Allow 4-6 weeks for delivery.
This offer is subject to withdrawal without notice

RESISTANCE
TARGET: SAHARA
5

GREGORY ST. GERMAIN

A SIGNET BOOK
NEW AMERICAN LIBRARY
TIMES MIRROR

PUBLISHER'S NOTE

This novel is a work of fiction. Names, characters, places, and incidents are either the product of the author's imagination or, if real, are used fictitiously.

NAL BOOKS ARE AVAILABLE AT QUANTITY DISCOUNTS WHEN USED TO PROMOTE PRODUCTS OR SERVICES. FOR INFORMATION PLEASE WRITE TO PREMIUM MARKETING DIVISION, THE NEW AMERICAN LIBRARY, INC., 1633 BROADWAY, NEW YORK, NEW YORK 10019.

Copyright © 1983 by C/B Concepts, Inc.

All rights reserved

The first chapter of this book appeared in *Road of Iron*, the fourth volume of this series.

SIGNET TRADEMARK REG. U.S. PAT. OFF. AND FOREIGN COUNTRIES
REGISTERED TRADEMARK—MARCA REGISTRADA
HECHO EN CHICAGO, U.S.A.

SIGNET, SIGNET CLASSIC, MENTOR, PLUME, MERIDIAN AND NAL BOOKS are published by The New American Library, Inc., 1633 Broadway, New York, New York 10019

First Printing, December, 1983

1 2 3 4 5 6 7 8 9

PRINTED IN THE UNITED STATES OF AMERICA

CHAPTER ONE

GIDEON'S INNER ALARM sounded. He was being followed.

The pandemonium of Cairo's labyrinthine streets had distracted him. They were packed with all types of people, who jostled him as he passed—countless shapes, colors, and nationalities in motley styles of dress, from Arabic robes to the latest Western fashions to military uniforms. Through the throngs rolled all kinds of vehicles—Egyptian gharries and mule carts, British lorries, and American Packards.

Variegated buildings lined the maze of streets—patchwork shops and stalls, mosques with slender minarets and bulbous domes, whitewashed villas, and multistoried office buildings. The odors of olive oil, incense, tobacco, hashish, sweat, garbage, and dung assailed his nose as the khamsin, the hot and dusty desert wind from the Sahara to the south, played against the cool breeze from the River Nile just to the west of the city.

It was the emergence of a pattern from the uproar around him that had finally alerted Gideon's dulled senses: the same faces again and again, the same car. He was certain of it: He was being passed along between tails. And not all of them were Egyptians. One of the persistent tag team was definitely European.

Christ, he thought, I don't need this now. His unexpected trip from England with In'Hout had been grueling and dangerous—plane to Malta, boat to Port Said, then train to Cairo. Gideon had slept only four hours the entire trip. The only other respite had been a couple of cold beers, a hot bath, and a three-course meal at Shepheard's, the Swiss-operated hotel where Philaix—the founder of the Phoenix commando team that Gideon headed—had arranged for him and In'Hout to stay.

And now he was being followed in a city where he shouldn't be known from Adam. And he was unarmed.

He still had a good distance to shake whoever his tails were. Philaix was staying at a villa in the Garden City suburb near GHQ, General Headquarters of the British High Command. In his urgent communiqué to Gideon in England, Philaix had asked for discretion once the Phoenix commander and In'Hout were in Cairo. Now Gideon knew why. In spite of the heavy British presence, Cairo's wide mix of people and points of view and its strong undercurrent of international intrigue existed still in July of 1941. There were obviously Axis spies about, and some of them were on to Gideon.

He cut quickly through an alley that doubled as a souk, crossed a narrow street, and entered a shop selling silks and ostrich plumes.

"Sabah el-kheir," the small wizened brown-faced proprietor greeted him, then launched into a hard sell in broken English.

Gideon, watching the street to see if his pursuers had spotted his dodge, bought some time by playing the bargaining game for a while. He saw none of the men from before, which proved nothing, since the tail might now be a new one. When he saw an empty taxi approaching, he dashed out of the store, waved it down, and hopped in.

Gideon spotted no one following while the young fez-topped Egyptian driver crisscrossed the old city. Finally, Gideon got out of the cab at the edge of the Garden City suburb.

He knew exactly where the villa was on the map of Cairo he had memorized during the long trip from England, but he took a circuitous route to be certain he had shaken the tail.

The villa was surrounded by a high stone wall. He rang the bell next to the ornate wrought-iron fence and waited. In a moment, Philaix himself, wearing his usual chalk-striped suit and paisley tie, crossed the courtyard from the large limestone house and let him in. With a quick nod of greeting, the aging, aristocratic Belgian industrialist led Gideon along the flagged bougainvillea-lined walkway, through an arched doorway and past the massive carved wooden door. They proceeded in silence along a dark hallway hung with goldleaf-framed portraits of pashas, and into a plush sitting room. There Philaix bade Gideon sit down on a divan covered in burgundy velvet. The older man took a seat on a straight-backed wooden chair opposite. There was a marble-topped table between them. On the table was a map.

"I'm glad you made it here safely," Henri Auguste Philaix said in his thickly accented English. "I hope your long voyage wasn't too tedious."

"It was all right," Gideon said. He didn't want to go into details, and Philaix didn't expect him to.

Philaix leaned forward without further preliminaries. "I know you've been following developments in the North Africa theater."

Gideon nodded.

"You are well aware that Germany has captured Libya. Ever since Rommel and his Afrika Korps took over from the Italian army—only five months ago, in February—the war here has been going their way. The British are just barely holding one last city in Libya—Tobruk—and are hard pressed to defend Egypt. German Panzers have now reached the Halfaya Pass on the border. Most of the action, as I'm sure you know, has been along the coastal road and the coastal plain, where the major North African cities and towns are located. The vast stretches of Saharan wilderness to the south have been for centuries the domain of only the desert nomads."

Philaix paused, his deep-set facial lines creasing even more. "That is, until now. I have a connection in the British High Command who was posted to Egypt two and a half months ago. Nine days ago, he contacted me—the day after I met with you at Bladesover about a possible mission in France. The day you rejoined the team training in Scotland, I flew to

Cairo. On my arrival, my friend informed me that mysterious reports have been coming from the Libyan desert. First, a patrol of the British LRDG, the Long Range Desert Group that specializes in Saharan navigation and reconnaissance, spotted a huge German supply convoy heading south along an apparently well-traveled route to the Great Sand Sea, an area where there was no previous report of a major military base. That area is here."

Philaix pointed to a sector on the large map in front of him. "It makes no sense that the Germans would mass troops in that area. Their military target is Egypt, and the terrain between the Great Sand Sea and the border is impassable."

"So what was the convoy doing?"

"We don't know. The LRDG tried to follow, but they were sighted and chased away by Messerschmitts. They barely escaped back to Egypt to report the incident. At approximately the same time, the British received some additional puzzling information from friendly Bedouins. These Arabs described seeing huge 'fountains of fire' shooting into the sky over the Great Sand Sea."

"Fountains of fire?" Gideon asked. "What the hell does that mean?"

"The obvious answer is some sort of weapons research and testing," Philaix said. "Important enough for the Germans to divert supplies, aircraft, and support troops away from their effort to drive the British from Egypt."

Gideon thought for a moment, then asked, "Have the British tried reconnaissance flights?"

"Yes," Philaix responded. "One was driven off by German fighters; the second never returned. And there won't be any more, I'm afraid. The British command is in disarray. Their latest counteroffensive, Operation Battleaxe, has been abandoned as a failure. As of today, Auchinleck has succeeded Wavell as commander in chief. His orders are to commit all his resources to defending the northern front. The British can't and won't devote a single plane or desert reconnaissance squad on what most of the command staff think is a wild-goose chase. My friend couldn't even convince them when we discovered further hard evidence of the mysterious site's importance—the discovery that led me to call you and In'Hout here suddenly."

Gideon leaned forward. "What evidence?"

"Four days ago, another Bedouin contact of ours—a man named Fuad El-Said—discovered a plane that had evidently crashed during a violent sandstorm in the area north of the Great Sand Sea. El-Said brought the bodies and papers of those killed in the crash across the border to the Siwa Oasis. The papers identified the men in the small Storch aircraft as the pilot, an SS security officer, and a civilian—Wolfgang Lichter, an Austrian research chemist."

"Research chemist," Gideon repeated. "That fits in with your theory about the mysterious facility."

"Exactly. On hearing this, I began to formulate a plan. You've demonstrated your skill at impersonation many times before, and you're a former chemistry scholar. I want you to assume the identity of Wolfgang Lichter in order to infiltrate the Nazi site. You and In'Hout will be escorted to the Siwa Oasis to meet El-Said. The Bedouin will lead both of you to the Great Sand Sea to search for the German base. When you find it, you'll go in as Lichter. In'Hout, whom I had come with you because he can pass most easily as an Arab, will scout the perimeter defenses and look for usable staging areas."

Gideon nodded. Joel In'Hout, the Dutch Jew who had been a gymnast and physical therapist before joining the elite Phoenix team, could carry off his deception fairly well. He asked, "What about the passage of time since the crash? Will the Germans be suspicious when Lichter suddenly appears?"

"It is certainly logical that Lichter would need time to recover from the crash before he could travel. He would also be forced to remain with the Bedouins, following their normal nomadic route until they happened on the site. I don't think the Germans would question his appearance."

"What if someone on the site knows Lichter personally?"

"That's a chance you'll have to take. I think the odds are with you, however, because he's Austrian, not German. Given the obvious importance of this facility, I consider the risk worth taking."

Gideon nodded, thinking again. "What happens after I find out what's going on at the site?"

"Then you get out the best way you can and rejoin In'Hout. You'll have a wireless, and you'll radio back to me. I will arrange for the rest of Phoenix to be parachuted to the drop site In'Hout selects. They'll bring with them the weaponry and explosives you determine are necessary to destroy the base, if you think it can be destroyed by a commando raid. If it requires a major military operation, you can return to Cairo and we'll try to persuade the British to move. But given the desperate situation on the northern front, I doubt if they would do anything."

"We've handled big jobs before," Gideon said. "And we can do it again." He stood. "When do we leave?"

"Tonight. The man I instructed In'Hout to meet with today—Chris Campbell, the liaison my friend in The British High Command has put at our disposal—will drive you to the Siwa Oasis. The route there will be westward along the coastal road as far as Mersa Matruh, then south along a desert track that bypasses the Qattara Depression."

Philaix outlined Gideon's route on the map on the table, then went on. "All your traveling will be at night. For one obvious reason—the deadly desert summer heat—and because there are spies everywhere, the very reason I wanted none of my help here today when I met with you."

"So it seems," Gideon agreed. "I was followed today."

Philaix's thick eyebrows rose. "Followed here?"

"No, I shook them."

"Arabs or Europeans?"

"Both."

"Why should they follow you?"

"A new face?" Gideon offered.

"Newcomers arrive every day on that same train from Port Said—fresh troops as well as civilian personnel—British and Anzacs. No, I don't like it. Be careful. Keep an eye out for a tail on leaving Cairo."

Philaix picked up and folded the map, then stood and moved to a desk, where he pulled out a single sheet of paper with columns of letters. He returned to Gideon.

"Take the map and the key to a code for your transmission. And take this with you, just in case."

The Belgian reached in his pocket, pulled out a German Mauser—a small 7.65mm handgun—and passed it to Gideon.

Gideon hefted it. "Thanks," he said.

"Would you like something before you go—some wine or beer perhaps?"

"Just some water."

"Of course."

Philaix disappeared to fetch bottled water. On his return, the two men talked for a little while about a joint British and Norwegian raid that March on the Lofoten Islands that had successfully destroyed six fish-oil plants related to explosives production and liberated three hundred Norwegian patriots. The Phoenix team which had gone to Norway the November before to destroy the iron-ore loading facilities at Narvik, had helped train the British commandos and Norwegian marines for the later raid.

Finally Philaix stood. "Monsieur Gideon, once again I offer you good luck."

Gideon shook his hand and left quickly. He decided to return to his hotel on foot. He had the rest of the afternoon before his departure, and although he was exhausted from the long journey, he felt too keyed up to sleep. He might as well get to know this city a little better, he thought.

He soon left the posh residential area behind and once again entered the narrow, rutted, dirty streets of the older commercial part of the city. There was striking difference now; the streets were almost eerily quiet, the merchants taking their midafternoon break during the hottest part of the day.

Cairo, Gideon marveled—a cluttered amalgam of old and new, like one giant bazaar in which he was also a display. Eyes peered out of doorways and windows at him as he passed by. He tried to see himself as the natives might—an informally dressed Westerner of medium but powerful build, with wavy brown hair, light hazel eyes, and a square jaw. He was probably considered an Anzac by them—Australian or New Zealander—rather than British.

Some of the dark mysterious eyes of the Egyptians seemed to see right into him. He wondered what they would make of his past—an American youth in upstate New York, reared as a Quaker; a rebellious college student, majoring in languages; a member of the Lincoln Brigade, fighting Fascism in the Spanish Civil War; a student of chemistry in Brussels; and Phoenix commander in Poland, Hungary, France, and Norway. A resistance fighter about to set out into the Great Sand Sea to run reconnaissance on "fountains of fire." Fortunately these probing eyes couldn't read his thoughts. . . .

Suddenly, two hands grabbed each of his arms, yanking him violently toward a doorway. Gideon smelled them first—a heavy oily scent of sweat and jasmine. Then he caught glimpses of them as he struggled—one in Western slacks and shirt, the other in a black burnous with a howli headdress, both of them dark-skinned. Gideon recognized the one in black as one of the men tailing him earlier in the day.

Gideon shouted for help, desperately looking up and down the street. All he saw was an empty parked car, a driver dozing in the cab of a parked vegetable truck, and rows of quiet shops. No one paid any attention to his struggle. The only other sound was a radio down the block, blaring a wailing Arabic sound.

For a moment, Gideon stopped struggling, letting his body go limp. Then with startling velocity he suddenly snapped both his elbows outward.

The two men, caught unawares, each took an elbow point in the lower throat and simutaneously lost their grip. Gideon sprinted to the left, barreling over one of the men, then dashed across the street.

A knife flew by him, low as if aiming for his legs, and stuck quivering into a sidewalk stool five feet in front of him.

Gideon whipped around, drawing his Mauser. He fired two quick shots. The robed man toppled dead onto the street.

Answering shots came from behind Gideon, then the

ominous, deadly chattering burst of an automatic weapon. Gideon darted right, then left, ramming his shoulder into a locked door. It didn't budge. He triggered a blind shot down the street, then headed for the truck. Bullets thudded into the vegetables above his head as he hit the pocked pavement under the vehicle.

The man with the machine pistol had sprinted from behind the parked car and was running toward him, firing as he came. Gideon rolled away from the stream of bullets ricocheting off the hard surface. In one lightning motion, he aimed and fired. The running man stopped in his tracks as if hit by a sledgehammer, then crashed head first onto the street.

Two dead, at least one more still in pursuit, as far as Gideon could tell.

The driver of the truck had ducked down below the windows. Gideon came up on the opposite side of the vehicle from his pursuer and swung open the door.

The driver was huddled up, terrified. Gideon, waving his gun, pushed him out of the way and slid behind the wheel. He found the ignition, turned it, and, depressing the clutch, slammed the truck into gear. Bullets ripped into the door's metal as Gideon hit the gas pedal, gunning the engine.

The Arab next to him, his eyes wide with fright, was ranting to Gideon in Arabic, pleading, begging. Gideon looked in the rear-view mirror. He saw a man take aim and fire a shot at the speeding truck, then jump into the parked car. Another man climbed in on the passenger side.

Damnation! There were still at least two more. And in a car.

Gideon accelerated through the narrow streets, skidding around sharp turns. At one corner the high truck rose off two wheels and nearly rolled, leaving crates of vegetables behind.

"Please!" The Egyptian at Gideon's side found the right English word, his hands clasped as if in prayer.

Gideon checked the mirror again. The car was still with him.

"Okay, here," Gideon said, tapping the brakes and grabbing the man's hands and pulling them toward the steering wheel.

The truck skidded slightly, but the man regained control. Gideon opened the door, stepped out onto the running board, and jumped. His feet went out from under him and he rolled along the gritty sidewalk, skinning flesh up and down one side.

He came up shooting at the car. The driver hadn't seen his jump and kept going past him after the truck. Gideon's first shot shattered a side window and the second hit the driver in the face. The car veered out of control up onto the opposite sidewalk and smashed into a streetlight.

Gideon started running. He saw an alley and turned left into it. Now there was a stone wall. He pulled himself up over it. He heard footsteps behind him.

More pursuers? Where the hell were they coming from? It was as if the streets were spewing them forth.

Gideon found himself in a courtyard. He tried the back door of a house. Locked. There were iron gates over the first-floor windows.

He headed for the wall on the far side of the yard. He looked over his shoulder. There were three men in the courtyard with him. He shot at one, dropping him, then clambered up the wall.

Hands grabbed his right ankle. He kicked his leg out and pulled himself up over the wall, clearing the jagged top. He was in another courtyard. He crouched low along the wall. When a head appeared from the other side, he shot, slicing through the man's neck. The head disappeared. He waited another moment for the third man. No one came. Gideon took off, climbing up over one more wall.

When he landed on the other side, he found himself on a wide well-populated street. Heads turned to look at him because of his dramatic arrival, but no one made any move toward him. He pocketed his Mauser, but kept his hand on it. There was a bar with an English name down the street—the Sweet Melody Club.

Gideon walked fast toward the bar, staying close to the shelter of doorways, checking over his shoulder for pursuers.

Suddenly, a huge arm reached out from one of the doorways and grabbed his throat, pulling him off the street. He tried to take out his gun, but a second man appeared and gripped him from the other side. Gideon stumbled and fell. He was dragged and pushed into a vestibule.

Gideon tensed, trying to prepare one last escape effort. Then he felt the cold steel of a long curved knife press against his neck and slide along it, drawing a line of blood.

"Don't move, not at all," a voice said in a British accent with a trace of something else—German, it had to be German. "I know who you are, Scott Gideon, and I want to talk with you."

Then a powerful blow struck the side of his head.

Gideon blacked out.

CHAPTER TWO

SLOWLY REGAINING CONSCIOUSNESS, Gideon became aware of the bouncing. He was hot and cramped, and he hurt all over—his head, his neck, his ribs. He opened his heavy eyelids and saw total darkness; he tried to extend his legs, but his feet struck metal. Gideon lifted his head and shook it to clear away the fog. He heard the whine of an engine and smelled the noxious odor of exhaust fumes.

He was in the trunk of a car.

With this realization, Gideon snapped fully awake. His mind raced over the events leading up to the blow to his head and his imprisonment. Someone—a German agent, it had to be—wanted to interrogate him. The Germans probably wanted to know why Gideon was in Cairo. Well, at least he'd be kept alive until the interrogation was over.

He probed around him and felt the metal contours of the trunk. Fingering the latch, he strained to spring the lock, with no success. He felt a spare tire, but found no tire iron or any other tool that could be used as a weapon.

He'd have to wait it out. Wait out the heat and the fumes.

He thought about the rest of the Phoenix team. They'd probably be training at Bladesover Manor in England right now, waiting for word from Gideon. They'd be without a leader soon if he didn't get out of this one. Brusilov, the war-tested Russian, would be the logical choice for a successor, Gideon thought, then Charvey; he was a former secretary of the International Federation of Transport Workers—he knew how to handle men. But the hell with that! I'll escape, Gideon resolved, clenching his teeth.

Finally, the car came to a halt. Gideon heard three doors slam and three sets of footsteps. A key was inserted into the lock, and as the trunk lid popped open, Gideon gulped for fresh air.

He saw three heads looming over him and three weapons—a Luger, a British Sten submachine gun, and a long curved knife.

Gideon could see in the moonlight that one of the men had cropped ruddy-blond hair and Aryan features. He looked vaguely familiar. Behind him were two robe-cloaked Arabs.

"Get out," the blond man said in the slightly accented English Gideon had heard before he'd been knocked out.

Gideon hauled himself out of the trunk and over the back of the car. His feet touched the sand, and he turned to face his captor.

Suddenly, a heavy boot swung viciously upward and caught Gideon in the groin, sending a violent stab of pain through him. He doubled over and fell to the ground.

"That's partial repayment for the Castle of the Polish Kings," the Aryan said. "You can be sure there is more to come."

Gideon regained his breath. Raging inside, he looked up and studied the face of his tormentor.

"Do you recognize me?" the man asked.

Now Gideon remembered: The young Waffen SS captain in Krakow who had supervised Gideon's excruciating torture. Gideon and the rest of the Phoenix team had escaped and successfully completed their mission, the rescue of General Kúznierz, now leader of the Polish resistance movement.

The German officer read the recognition on Gideon's face. "That's right, Gideon. My name is von Briel. Your escape nearly ruined my career. Fortunately, my linguistic skills were needed here in North Africa. I have had my successes behind enemy lines, too."

"No doubt with little Arab boys," Gideon hissed.

The German kicked out with his boot, again catching

Gideon in the groin. Gideon sagged to his knees and vomited. Von Briel watched him for a moment, barked an order in Arabic to his two accomplices, and started off. The two Arabs grabbed Gideon under the arms, roughly pulled him upright, and thrust him forward. He staggered behind the German, struggling to keep up.

The pain gradually eased enough for Gideon to look up. Ahead, three immense triangular shapes filled the desert landscape, silhouetted in their vastness against the pitch-black sky. They were the pyramids near Cairo—those of Khufu, Khafre, and Menkaure—three giant tombs constructed of millions of massive stone blocks. And close by to the east stood the Sphinx, its battered face impassively keeping watch on one of the nearly million nights since the monument had been carved.

Gideon wondered if a perverse sense of history had led von Briel to bring him southwest of the city to interrogate and kill him, entombing him in the same desert sands that served as the sacred burial ground of the Egyptians. He briefly considered lunging for von Briel, but the Arabs behind him would cut him down before he got a step. He'd wait for a better chance.

They moved along a stone walkway to the base of the towering pyramid of Khufu. At 450 feet, the tallest of the three pyramids loomed over the human figures below.

"Stop," the German ordered. He nodded to the Arabs. Each man untied his *agal*, the goat's-hair coil that held the traditional *keffiyeh* head shawl in place. One man began tying Gideon's hands behind his back with his coil, while the other bound his ankles.

While they were working, von Briel stood in front of Gideon, smirking. "You'll soon wish—"

Gideon spit in his face.

The German's features twisted in rage and disgust. He punched Gideon square on the chin, slamming him backward into the coarse stone base of the ancient pyramid.

Von Briel gestured angrily to one of the Arabs, who handed him a horsehair-tipped whip, with which he lashed the back of Gideon's neck, drawing blood. Gideon grunted in pain and twisted his head to face the Nazi.

"You're going to kill me anyway," Gideon panted. "Get on with it."

"Tell me what you are doing in Cairo. And why you have a map of the desert and the key to some sort of code."

Gideon shifted slightly as the German talked. The Arab hadn't completed the knot on his hands when von Briel had punched him. Already, he'd loosened the goat's-hair cord by working his wrists. If he could stall for enough time, he might be able to work free. But he'd have to be careful; the two Arabs' dark eyes were fixed on him.

Gideon remained silent.

A humorless smile came to von Briel's face. He handed the whip back to the Arab, lit a cigarette, and took a deep drag. Exhaling, he held the cigarette toward Gideon.

"V cigarettes," he said. "India tobacco. A good brand, the choice of most of the British officers I meet. But they do have a tendency to burn too hot, *nicht wahr*?"

The German suddenly bent down and touched the burning tip of the cigarette to the raised whip welt on Gideon's neck. Gideon jerked his head away and tried to roll. He yanked hard against his bonds and felt the goat's-hair cord give more.

"Is it worth the pain?" von Briel asked. "Why are you in Egypt? To meet with the British High Command?"

Gideon didn't reply.

Von Briel burned him again, this time on the earlobe. A groan escaped through Gideon's clenched teeth.

"The next time it goes inside the ear," the German said. "Think of it, Gideon. The pain is unlike anything you can imagine." He took a drag on the cigarette, then asked again, "Did you meet with the British High Command?"

"Yes," Gideon lied, buying time to work on his bonds. The Arabs were getting bored and their eyes had begun to drift.

"Why would they be interested in an American-led commando team? Their own desert raiders have been quite effective."

"Why do you think?"

Von Briel grabbed the front of Gideon's shirt with his left hand and held the cigarette just off Gideon's left ear with his right hand. "I've had enough smart remarks, Gideon. This is the last warning. Why did the High Command want to meet with you?"

Gideon looked at him for a moment, then sighed exaggeratedly and said, "They wanted me to go on a fox hunt."

"I warned you—"

"The Desert Fox," Gideon added quickly. "They wanted me to kill Rommel."

Von Briel let go of Gideon. As the Phoenix leader fell back, he tugged hard at his bonds almost pulling his wrists free.

Von Briel thought for a moment. "If you're going to kill Rommel, why do you have a map of the desert?"

"We'd escape through the desert," Gideon answered. "Back to our staging area."

"Where is that?"

"Hold the map up."

The German unfolded the map Gideon had been carrying.

"I can't see," Gideon said.

As the German leaned forward, Gideon's hands pulled free. He grabbed von Briel's left wrist, jerked him off balance, then hit him in the throat with the fingertips of his stiffened right hand, smashing his larynx. Gideon yanked the luger from his unfastened holster.

The Arabs hesitated; the German was in their line of fire. Gideon drilled one in the abdomen, and a Sten flew out of his hands. As Gideon spun toward the second, he saw the flash of steel in the moonlight just in time to shove von Briel forward. The long knife sliced through the German's chest, and he crumpled to the ground. Gideon shot the Arab in the face.

Then he grabbed the scimitar and cut the cord binding his feet. Flinching with pain, he knelt and rifled through the dead German's pockets, retrieving his Mauser, the map, and the key to the code. He also found the keys to the Fiat and a spare clip for the Luger. He started for the beat-up car.

He had almost reached it when shots rang out. The first Arab he had shot still had enough life in him to pick up the Sten, prop himself up, and trigger a burst. But the wounded man shot wide, and the bullets ripped into the front of the car. Gideon pivoted, firing back two shots with the Luger. The man took a bullet in the neck and fell prone again.

Gideon checked the sedan for damage. Both front tires were flat, and water was spouting from three holes in the radiator, forming murky puddles in the sand. He swore. It was going to be a long walk back to Cairo.

Gideon followed the Nile northward to the city along a paved road past rows of lebbek trees. In the distance, near the water, he saw occasional dots of light—oil lamps flicking in the windows of fellahin shacks of peasants still awake despite their long day of farm labor. He heard donkeys braying, and he could barely see in the moonlight the large shapes of grazing water buffalo. There were boats on the river even at this time—exotic feluccas with triangular sails, transporting their various cargoes, like giant one-winged birds skimming the glassy surface.

The trek took three long, painful hours. The desert was cold as the sand shed the day's heat. With the chill, his painful neck wounds, and hordes of bothersome mosquitoes, it was all he could do to keep going.

Gideon reached Shepheard's just after one a.m. Five people still lounging around the lobby turned to gawk at the bedraggled American as he stopped at the front desk for his keys, then wearily climbed the plushly carpeted stairs to his room.

In'Hout was waiting for him. The small wiry Dutchman had probably walked the same distance as Gideon in the same time span, but his hike had been in the confines of the room, pacing like a caged cat.

"Where have you been? What the hell happened?" In'Hout asked.

Gideon told his story betwen huge gulps of icewater.

"My God," In'Hout remarked. "A close one. And all because a Kraut agent had a good memory for faces."

"At least it's over," Gideon said. "When do we leave?"

"As soon as you're ready. The truck is loaded. Our British liaison is waiting for my call." In'Hout moved toward the phone.

Gideon groaned to himself. He'd been looking forward to a night's sleep, but the mission came first.

"Tell him an hour," Gideon said. "I've got to have a shower and a meal."

Chris Campbell, a Scotsman, drove a two-ton lorry with In'Hout seated next to him and Gideon riding shotgun. Campbell was an easygoing sort, happy to answer their questions about Egypt, Libya, and desert life. He had two great hates—Nazis and office politics. And he had two great loves—women and Scotch whisky. He claimed to be delighted to be out of the office—he worked for Philaix's connection at GHQ—and on a field trip, where he could make use of skills he had picked up as High Command liaison to the LRDG.

After heading northwest for a stretch, they turned westward at Alexandria and followed the beautiful road through El Alamein and El Daba. On their right was the Mediterranean Sea, silvery blue in the moonlight; on their left was a vast sandy plain stretching endlessly into the night.

The sun was rising as they neared Mersa Matruh. Here the road was jammed in both directions with military traffic—light Vickers tanks, heavy cruiser tanks, armored scout cars, supply lorries, and ambulance convoys. An occasional Egyptian shepherd, looking completely out of place amid the military hustle and bustle, lounged sedately under a portable awning, while his flock nibbled at the sparse growth.

The small flat village of Mersa Matruh, already engulfed in the first of the day's heat, consisted of a collection of white buildings with sun-dried brick walls, surrounded by tents of both Bedouin and military design. Commerce was already in full swing and Campbell had to wind his way carefully through the cluttered, noisy streets.

Their original plan had been to cut southwestward on the desert track from Mersa Matruh toward Siwa Oasis before first light, to avoid detection by enemy agents. Now, because of the trouble caused by Gideon's capture, they had no choice but to risk leaving in daylight. Campbell's suggestion that they have a decent breakfast at the Ship Inn before departure met with no arguments from Gideon or In'Hout.

Gideon, gazing out the lorry window, noticed a house constructed of discarded oil cans. A big, faded blue 1934 Chevy was parked in front of the house. Three *hadar*, or townspeople, who were working on the car lifted their heads out from under the hood to watch the truck roll by.

Campbell parked the lorry directly opposite the inn, so they could keep an eye on it from the arcaded patio. They had just begun their breakfast of eggs, toast, and yogurt when a tall, redheaded man in khaki shirt and shorts approached. He greeted Campbell, who introduced the man as Greg Noonan, an Irishman.

"Have you lads heard? Word's just come through. Germany invaded Russia."

The three men sat motionless for a moment as the news sunk in. The call of a muezzin from a minaret, beckoning people to the mosque, filled the silence.

Then Campbell spoke. "Goddam Hitler. He's a bloody lunatic."

"That he is," Noonan consented. "But one more front for the Jerries might help us here—one more front they have to supply."

Gideon thought of Brusilov, wondering how the Russian would take the news. A former Royal Cadet, he hated the Bolsheviks. Now his former enemies were his allies against Nazism.

After finishing breakfast, they headed out of town under a now blazing-hot sun. Passing the oil-can house, Gideon noticed the absence of the blue Chevy. Whatever the problem had been, the men had fixed it.

The 200-mile desert track to the Siwa Oasis was no more than a narrow strip of gravelly sand packed firmly enough to support heavy vehicles. Campbell had made the taxing trip twice before, he said, both times at night. Now with the full force of the desert heat upon them it would be that much more arduous. They passed through rocky hills and over stretches of sandy wastes. As the sun climbed higher in the sky the air seemed to shimmer pink in the haze, highlighting the barren dun-colored vistas. The cab of the lorry was like an oven, worse than the 110-degree heat outside. From time to time Campbell would park the truck in the shade of an acacia tree or a hillock to let the engine cool off. The passengers would take sips from the water jugs and wipe the dusty sweat off their faces before starting out again.

At one of these stopovers, Campbell pointed out another vehicle to the north—just a speck on the horizon. It stayed the same size for a good five minutes.

"It stopped when we stopped. It's following us, unless you believe in coincidences."

Gideon shook his head. "But let's make sure. If it is a tail, we want to deal with it before Siwa. Can we leave the track here?"

"Yes. There's a layer of rock under the sand sheet to the east, so we should be all right. I have rope ladders and steel channels to free the wheels from soft sand if necessary."

"Good."

The Scot thought for a moment. "I have an idea. If it does prove to be a tail, we can lead them southward toward the Qattara Depression. There are fissures and escarpments along its rim where we can hide. Afterward, we can pick up the track that leads from the depression to Siwa. We won't be going too far out of the way."

"Let's go," Gideon said.

They climbed back into the lorry's hot cab. After a mile they left the track and cut due south, stopping for a moment to let In'Hout climb around to the back to serve as a lookout, then continued on their way, the truck banging and jouncing over the rugged terrain.

In'Hout knocked on the back of the cab after three more miles, having spotted the vehicle still following the lorry's tire marks across the desert floor. It was the Chevy, In'Hout could now see. Gideon was dismayed but not surprised.

Sun-seared and dust-scoured, they reached the Qattara Depression three hours later. They'd had to stop several times either to remove loose rocks from their path or to place the ladders or channels under their tires. To Campbell's surprise, the Chevrolet had managed to stay with them in spite of the rough ground.

"I see a hiding spot," Campbell said. He pulled the lorry into a fissure near the chasm's edge, then ran back to wipe away their tracks. Gideon chose a concealed vantage point on top of an escarpment where they could watch the approaching vehicle. They took a Sten submachine gun and grenades with them.

While they waited, Campbell described the remarkable landform called the Qattara Depression. The chasm, 140 miles long and as much as 75 miles wide, was located in the geographic center of Egypt. The depression had probably been an inland sea. There was a huge salt bog at its bottom, 1,000 feet below sea level, the lowest point in Africa. They could make out a descending series of cliffs and rocks a good part of the way down, but toward the bottom they could see only a shimmering pink haze.

Gideon turned his attention to the northwest as the blue Chevrolet slowly approached.

"Who are those bastards?" he muttered.

Ten minutes later the Chevy pulled up to the edge of the depression where the lorry tracks ended and the same three men from Mersa Matruh, dressed in galabiyas and skullcaps, climbed out. They were obviously confused, looking down the depression, then at the ground for tracks, then toward the escarpment.

"Do we take them?" In'Hout asked.

"If they're spying for the Germans, I'd like to take them alive," Campbell replied. "I'm sure M16 would love to know who their contact is."

"Okay, then," Gideon said, "let's show them there's no way home."

He stood up suddenly, shouted a warning, pulled the pin from a grenade, and tossed it toward the car as the Arabs scattered. The grenade bounced against the front left tire and detonated, sending shards of metal and glass in all directions with a jagged flash of light that was followed by a second explosion of the gas tank in the rear.

One of the men had been knocked down by the impact. He staggered up and, running toward the escarpment, pulled a grenade from under his robe. He heaved a German "potato masher" that bounced at In'Hout's feet. The Dutchman kicked out with his right foot, knocking it about fifteen feet away, and dove to the ground as the grenade exploded.

"Christ," Gideon swore as he jumped to his feet. "That was too fucking close."

He grabbed the Sten and let loose two short bursts toward the man below, who had pulled out a pistol. The man got off only one harmless shot before 9mm slugs slammed into his head and neck, killing him instantly.

Gideon pivoted toward the other two men, who had crouched behind the car, which was pouring out black oily smoke. He fired a burst into the air. One man moved into view, waving a handkerchief as a white flag.

Gideon, In'Hout, and Campbell wound their way down from their perch, guns ready, watching for sudden moves. With a wave of the Sten's barrel, Gideon directed the two Arabs away from the heat of the burning car and into the shade below the face of the escarpment. They hurried along, hands pointing to the sky, their eyes wide and frightened.

In'Hout collected their knives and handguns—both of them Webleys, probably stolen from British soldiers—as Campbell talked to them in Arabic. At first they were monosyllabic, but when Campbell became irate and threatening, they quickly opened up, babbling in the gargled sounds of their language.

The Scot turned to the others. "That didn't take long. The idea of a long desert walk in their birthday suits got them to talk. I already have the name of their contact and the time and place of their next meeting, assuming they're telling the truth."

"Why were they following us?" Gideon demanded.

"They were told to watch for anyone heading south out of Mersa Matruh. They would have followed us all the way to Siwa to see if we were going into Libya."

"Ask them what's so important in the south. Why just the south?"

Campbell did so, listened to the answer, then reported, "They swear on Allah they don't know. I believe them."

"Ask them to speculate."

The Scot and the Arabs talked back and forth for several minutes more, then Campbell translated. "They assume it has something to do with troop movements and a coming invasion of Egypt. That's why they're helping the Germans. They want the English out of Egypt. Other pro-German villagers along the coast also have been instructed to watch the southern routes. I'll tell you one thing for certain—whatever the Jerries are doing in the southern desert, it's got to be big, damn big, because they're obviously going to a hell of a lot of trouble to find out if we know about it."

CHAPTER THREE

"THERE IT IS, Siwa Oasis. You can see the rim of cliffs surrounding it." Chris Campbell pointed with his right hand.

Gideon and In'Hout peered through the windshield at the shapes on the horizon. The final leg of desert track led up to a pass through the rocks. They followed it, once beyond the pass, and found themselves overlooking an island of life.

Siwa sat in a depression below the cliffs, a sunken garden of trees—date palm, pomegranate, lime, and olive—some sixty feet below sea level. There were also dwellings—white limestone houses and brown mud huts—in and around which people went about their day's work. Even a few domestic animals were evident. Concentric walls of mud and palm branches encircled a water hole.

"Those walls were built to protect the precious *bir*—the well—from dust and sandstorms," Campbell remarked.

Gideon thought about the oases depicted on his map of the western Sahara. Where there were a lot of Germans, there had to be a source of water, unless they were trucking everything in. Their mystery site might well be located at an oasis.

"Are all of the oases mapped?" he asked.

"Most of them. The Bedouin are naturally close-mouthed about them. Each one can support only so much life. The oases determine tribal orbits. We've done some mapping from the air. Most oases aren't as lush as Siwa, but where there is water, there are usually date palms. In fact, it's usually the palms that show the Bedouin where to look for water. Their roots seek out the water table beneath the desert floor, where faults in the rock allow subterranean moisture to travel upward toward the surface."

They drove carefully down the path and entered the tiny village. Their first stop was at the small British post to deliver their prisoners. Gideon and In'Hout lifted the two bound men out of the back of the lorry while Campbell reported the incident. When the Scot returned, he suggested dinner.

"When do we rendezvous with our guide?" Gideon asked.

"He's camped somewhere on the edge of the desert. He no doubt already knows we're here; everyone at Siwa must. He'll find us when you're ready to leave, just after dark."

Campbell knew of a canteen run by a Greek that was usually well stocked with liquor and food. Leaving the truck at the post, they walked past tall palms and sun-parched huts to the small establishment.

They sat outside on palm-wood chairs pulled up to a table under a thatch awning. Both the Greek proprietor and his Levantine wife came over to take their order. The men started with Scotch, then moved on to Stella beer with their meal of lamb and couscous. As an after-dinner drink, they ordered *lagmi*, a liquor made from the fermented sap of the date palm.

From their seats, mellowed by the food and drink, they watched a brilliant sunset that drenched the desert in crimson and rose. At dusk, the wind picked up, rustling the long spindly leaves of the palms. The Greek proprietor moved quietly from table to table, lighting oil lamps as darkness descended, bringing with it a blessed coolness.

Suddenly, a big man appeared out of the shadows. Gideon and In'Hout instinctively tensed, but Chris Campbell stood with a smile of recognition on his ruddy Scottish face.

The man moved silently into the light cast by the lamp. He had a bearded, aquiline face with a long hooked nose and wore a black turban, a long white shirt, olive-green pantaloons, a black *aba* overcoat, and embroidered riding boots with upturned toes. Over his shoulder he carried a Reveilli, a 6.5mm Italian rifle; a long curved knife was stuck in his belt.

Campbell introduced the man as Fuad El-Said.

Gideon and In'Hout stood and shook hands. The Bedouin then turned.

"See that clump of trees over there? Bring your supplies. I will be waiting." His voice was deep and, surprisingly, his English was tinged with a British accent rather than an Arabic one.

Gideon nodded, and the Bedouin disappeared into the shadows as quickly and quietly as he'd appeared.

Campbell laughed. "I think we should all be glad he's on our side.

They paid their bill in pounds, then headed for the lorry and drove to the clump of pines, to which were tied four camels. Said stood a few paces away, calmly gazing at the nighttime sky. He turned to watch as the Westerners began unloading supplies from the back of the truck—Sten guns, ammunition, tins of bully beef, boxes of biscuits, packets of pressed dates, and the wireless radio in its protective metal valise.

The Bedouin wrapped all the gear in blankets and loaded it onto the camels. Although most of it went into a *bassour*, a wicker palanquin strapped to the pack camel, each man would carry water, weapons, and ammo on his own mount. Gideon secured Wolfgang Lichter's documents, with In'Hout carrying the map and code book.

Said handed them each a bundle. "Desert clothes," he said.

They were changing when Campbell remembered something, ran back to the lorry, and returned with a package. He passed it to Gideon, saying, "Lichter's undergarments, to make your deception complete. They're even freshly laundered."

Gideon smiled. "Philaix thinks of everything."

Following Said's instructions, Gideon and In'Hout donned the multiple layers of Bedouin clothing, including an elaborate head shawl that was difficult to adjust properly.

When they were ready to go, Said turned to Campbell. "I know everyone in the oasis, and tonight there are no new faces. We should be safe, but these are uncertain times. Watch to see if we are followed. If so, report it to the post before you leave. They can radio us."

Campbell agreed. Gideon and In'Hout thanked the genial Scot for his help and following the Bedouin's lead, mounted the camels. In'Hout, the former professional acrobat, had no trouble pulling himself up into the high saddle, but Gideon needed a second attempt to get the awkward maneuver right.

They set off across a rocky plain into the desert night. The black-domed sky was filled with a glittering starscape, dimmed only slightly when a bright sliver of moon broke over the horizon. With the lack of moisture in the air—and thus no insulating blanket of clouds—the heat continued to dissipate until the temperature had dropped fifty degrees. Gideon, at first uncomfortable in the bulky Bedouin clothing, was happy to have the camel-hair burnous for warmth. In the day's heat, Said explained, the many layers served to keep the coolness in. That, Gideon thought, might take some getting used to. Even the crude camel-leather boots, soled with rubber from discarded tires, felt comfortable now.

They made good time, the camels maintaining a steady pace, though the two Phoenix members rocked and swayed and bobbed uncomfortably with the jarring motion. Gideon tried talking to his one-humped dromedary, with no discernible result. He had read once that camels, unlike horses, were ill-tempered and treacherous.

"Does my camel have a name?" he called ahead to their guide.

Said looked back over his shoulder. "No. The Bedouin rarely names his camels. That way they are easier to eat when they falter."

"Is that why they're so damned haughty?" In'Hout joked.

Said laughed. "Some say it's because they know how much the Bedouin needs them. But it is also said that Allah has a hundred wonderful names, of which man knows ninety-nine. Only the camel knows the hundredth."

After several grueling hours, the Bedouin signaled a halt and all dismounted. They had arrived at "the Wire," the metal fence running along the wilderness border between Egypt and Libya. Said led them on foot a few hundred yards to the south until they encountered a break in the barrier through which they crossed onto Libyan soil. They stopped for a brief period to restore their bodies with rest and water.

They rode the rest of the night, falling into a semiconscious state just short of sleep. With the morning's first rays of light, they reached a stretch of *serir*, "desert pavement," a formation of bare rock polished by wind and sand. Said led them to a shelter under a topheavy "pedestal rock" that had been eroded away at the base by blowing sand.

When the sun broke over the horizon, it was a huge orange sphere. For a moment, the entire eastern desert seemed to be on fire. Gideon thought of the "fountains of fire" reported by the Bedouins. As his goal approached, he felt the familiar tension rising within him.

When Said had finished hobbling the four camels, he turned to face the east, stooped, touched the ground with the palms of his hands, passed them over his arms and face as if washing, then sat in silent meditation for a moment. He launched into his prayer—first standing, then sitting, then dipping his forehead to the ground. He turned his head to the right and the left, intoning first in Arabic, *"La ilaha, illah Allah; Mohammed rasul Allah,"* and then in English, "There is but one God and Mohammed is his prophet." The Bedouin sat in another moment of meditation. His body relaxed and his eyes glazed over.

"Four times a day," In'Hout whispered under his breath.

"Come," Said suddenly ordered as if the others had been dawdling. "We will set up the tent before it gets much hotter."

The tent consisted of a black haircloth blanket stretched over wooden poles that formed an oblong pitched roof with drooping ends. It was pegged down on three sides with guy ropes extending outward. The fourth side was left open facing downwind. Wool rugs served as a floor, with hard grain-stuffed cushions as pillows.

They ate some of their rations and sipped water before settling down to a hot, restless sleep.

Gideon woke to the sound of a crackling fire. In'Hout was on the other side of the tent, snoring. A lizard was perched on the Dutchman's arm. Gideon left it alone and crawled out the tent. By the sun's position in the sky, he saw that it was late afternoon, but it was still brutally hot. In spite of the heat and the hard rock on which they lay, Gideon and In'Hout had slept a long time—not surprising, considering how little rest they had been getting.

The Bedouin guide was brewing tea over a fire of scrub brush and camel dung. Gideon watched him pour the green liquid from the pot into cups, add sugar to each, and pour the liquid back into the pot. He repeated this process several times until the brew had a thick syrupy consistency.

While sipping at the hot drink, which proved refreshing in spite of its temperature, Gideon silently studied Fuad El-Said. He knew most Bedouins were not of original Egyptian or North African stock, but were descended from nomads who had begun crossing over out of Arabia a millennium ago, bringing the Arabic language and Muslim religion with them. Their alliances were to families, clans, and tribes, but not to nations. They belonged to the desert.

Gideon broke the silence. "Why have you joined the battle against the Nazis?"

The Bedouin looked up, met Gideon's eyes, and took another sip of tea. "After I answer I will ask you the same question. Many of my people consider this a European war fought on African soil, a war that little concerns our way of life. Before the Germans came, when the Italians were fighting the British, I agreed, since the Bedouin was still free."

"How did the Germans change this?" Gideon asked.

Said's rugged face creased into a look of hatred. "The Germans have an arrogance about them. They wish to impose their new order on all peoples, even the Bedouin, who do them no harm. Not content to take over the cities, they send their trucks and equipment into the Great Sand Sea, where we have lived for centuries. They must be stopped, and I will give my life to do it, *in sha Allah*, if God wills."

Gideon watched the Bedouin take another sip of tea. Then he asked, "How do you come to speak such good English, if you are a man of the desert?"

Said smiled. "My father was an enlightened man. He believed that I should be educated in many ways of life, so I could understand and choose between them. When I was a boy, he left me in the care of an English couple in Alexandria. I found the British often smug and pigheaded, and I learned that I could never live with them, that I would always be a man of the desert. Still, I believe the British are well-meaning and will eventually set us free. The Germans only wish to grind us into the desert sands. And you, American?"

"The German lust for conquest will eventually touch all peoples," Gideon said. "Americans as well as Bedouins."

In'Hout stepped out of the tent, stretched, and walked over to join the others.

At that instant, they heard the hum of an engine.

"Plane," Gideon said, rising, his first instinct to head for his Sten.

"Stay where you are," Said cautioned. "For all they've done, the Germans haven't yet started bombing the Bedouin."

In a moment, the three men saw the aircraft flying low in the sky. Said identified it as a Gibli, a small Italian reconnaissance plane. Slow but maneuverable, they were often used for German patrols, the Bedouin explained. Armed with two bombs and a machine gun, they were effective attack planes as well.

The Gibli passed overhead, heading south, then swung around in a wide arc and returned. It buzzed them again, loud and incredibly low, then disappeared to the north.

Gideon exhaled a sigh of relief.

Said stood up. "Let us break camp. We should reach the edge of the Great Sand Sea before the next light."

They packed up and moved out as the sun was setting, soon leaving the polished rock of the *serir* behind. The camels found surer footing in the soft sand, Said reported, and they would make better time.

Suddenly, they heard the distant but familiar sound of an airplane. The noise rapidly grew louder.

"It's coming back!" In'Hout yelled ahead to the others.

The Gibli passed low over the pedestal rock to their north, then banked sharply in their direction.

"Scatter!" Gideon shouted.

The three men, kicking the sides of their camels, spread out over the desert floor. Said led the fourth camel, the pack animal, by a rope.

The Italian plane, engine roaring, passed over where they had been together a moment before and dropped one of the bombs. Sand, shrapnel, and flame erupted into the sky.

Gideon, holding the reins with his left hand, reached down to grab the Sten gun out of its protective blanket with his right. The plane, scarcely twenty feet above the ground, was approaching from the west out of the setting sun. After the loud explosion the camel was skittish. Gideon let the reins go to pivot and fire at the approaching Gibli. At the gunshots, his animal panicked and broke into a run. Gideon lost his balance and toppled to the ground as machine-gun fire sounded.

He stood up, shaken, gripping the Sten tightly. The Gibli soared over him, still firing at the camel. Helpless, Gideon watched the camel fall to the sand with a horrible noise.

Said had dismounted and was firing at the plane with his Reveilli. In'Hout was next to his camel, Sten over his shoulder, digging frantically in his pack. The panic-stricken animal was jerking its head back and forth wildly, and In'Hout just managed to grab a flare gun and two flares before the animal broke into a frantic run and joined the two remaining camels.

The Gibli had swung around for another pass. In'Hout, Gideon, and Said hit the sand, forming a wide triangle on the desert floor, with the terrified camels in the middle.

The plane swept by, machine gun spitting bullets as it

dropped a second bomb onto the animals. One darted away in time, but flame and metal ripped into the other two, and they collapsed into a blackened mess of blood and gore.

Gideon and In'Hout loosed full clips at the plane. Bullets perforated the Gibli's tail, with no effect, as it banked for a fourth run.

Suddenly, In'Hout jumped up and started running to draw the plane's fire. The Gibli angled toward him, sweeping in for the kill, scarcely five yards off the ground. Its machine gun let loose a blistering hail of lead. The bullets kicked up the sand in a linear pattern which quickly moved closer and closer to the zigzagging man.

Just before the line of fire reached him, In'Hout leaped to one side, pointed the loaded signal flare gun upward, and fired at the plane's exposed belly.

The flare hit the Gibli's fuselage forward of the left wing and exploded. The pilot, startled by the intense phosphorescent flash, pulled the stick to the right, catching his wingtip on the top of a small dune. The Gibli flipped over wildly for several hundred yards, breaking up on the way. The fuselage burst into flames, and exploded as the fuel tank ignited. Jagged pieces of hot metal flew across the desert floor. What was left continued to burn, sending orange-blue flames and oily smoke roiling upward.

Gideon ran to In'Hout and clapped him on the shoulder. "Good thinking," he said.

The Dutchman nodded, and he and Gideon joined Said, who was staring at a wounded, bleating camel in anger and disgust.

The Bedouin raised his rifle. "It is written." With a single bullet, he ended the camel's suffering.

The three men turned to the other animals. Two were dead, and what they carried was destroyed. But the pack camel had survived, and with it most of their supplies. They still had half their water, small-arms ammunition, and a couple of grenades.

They paused for a moment to take some water. "Why do you think the plane attacked us?" Gideon asked Said.

"I have never heard of the Germans or Italians attacking Bedouin without provocation. I can think of only one reason— the order has been issued that absolutely no one is to be allowed anywhere near the Great Sand Sea."

Said's thoughts echoed Gideon's own.

CHAPTER FOUR

THEY WALKED ALL night, carrying their weapons. The one surviving camel, trailing on a rope behind Fuad El-Said, carried everything else.

They were seeing fewer and fewer rocks and less scrub. At sunrise Said informed them that they had already crossed over onto the vast area of sand known as the Great Sand Sea. The early-morning light gave the sand a reddish cast, but soon the sun, climbing higher in the sky, reflected off the ground in glaring buff-white hues. At first glance, it seemed as if the landscape stretched out endlessly in terrifying sameness—a huge ocean of sand rising and falling in wavelike dunes. But upon closer inspection, Gideon and In'Hout could see variation.

There were different dune patterns: the most common crescent-shaped "barchan" dunes, the longitudinal "sword" dunes, and the multisided "star" dunes, shaped by the driving Saharan wind—the khamsin.

The Bedouin pointed out the leeward slope of a long sword dune that would offer shelter from the dry wind, if not the sun, and they headed toward it.

He suddenly signaled them to stop. "The blue men are here as well," he said, staring at camel tracks in the sand. "Mehari trotting camels."

"The blue men?" Gideon asked.

"Yes, the Tuareg. They are called blue men because of their indigo-dyed robes and veils."

"Are they Bedouin?"

"They are nomads, but not of Arab stock. They are descended rather from the Berbers, an African line. We brought them Islam, but they do not speak Arabic. Their language is of the Hamitic group, not the Semitic. We also call them the pirates of the desert. They are camel raiders and slave traders. But they normally roam the desert far to the west of here. I don't know why they have come to the Great Sand Sea."

"Especially since the Germans and Italians are attacking other nomads in the area. Will the Tuareg be hostile to us?" Gideon asked.

Said's dark eyes narrowed. "Most definitely."

"So what do we do about them?"

"Let's hope that since they passed by here only recently, they won't be heading this way again. We'll set up camp here until dark, and sleep in shifts, taking turns on watch. I'll take the first watch. We must—"

"We're in trouble," In'Hout interrupted, his voice tight with tension. "Look!"

Gideon and Said spun around. Twelve Tuareg warriors mounted on camels lined the ridge of a dune to the west. They wore blue robes and black turbans, part of which covered their faces, revealing only their eyes. Most of them had long spears, swords, and shields of camel hide. Only two carried guns.

Gideon broke into a run, shouting, "Spread out! Get the ones with the rifles first!"

A spear sailed past his head and stuck in the sand behind him. A rifle cracked and a bullet just missed his boot. He whipped his Sten around into firing position.

The blue men had also spread out. Gideon spotted a warrior with a rifle galloping along the ridge of the dune. Stopping short, Gideon planted his feet firmly in the sand and fired from the hip.

His first burst caught the camel. Legs shot out from under it and the animal crashed to the sand. The rider rolled to one side. Gideon kept firing. The Tuareg didn't get up.

In'Hout and Said crouched twenty yards apart on the sand,

firing. Said's third shot tore away part of a blue man's face. In'Hout swept his Sten back and forth on full automatic, raking a group of three charging warriors. Two fell from their camels, but the third kept coming, slicing at In'Hout's head with his razor-sharp sword. In'Hout caught the blow with the barrel of his Sten, then triggered a burst. The dead man fell on top of him. While scrambling out from under the corpse, In'Hout pulled his only grenade off his belt and jumped up, running for his target, while cocking his arm for the throw.

Gideon had the same idea. Hearing a burst of rifle fire from one of the Tuareg, Gideon pulled the pin on his one grenade and heaved it.

The two grenades fell on either side of the warrior with the gun. Another blue man rode his camel over to reinforce the first, crossing the ground where Gideon's grenade rolled. A third Tuareg frantically tried to bat In'Hout's grenade away with his spear like a polo player.

The two explosions were almost simultaneous. Hot shrapnel ripped into men and camels. Three more Tuareg dead.

A warrior picked up the rifle of the first man Gideon had shot. Gideon quickly zeroed in on him and stitched a seam of blood across his chest.

Two warriors were bearing down on In'Hout with their spears. Gideon pivoted and, taking careful aim so as not to hit his comrade, shot at one of In'Hout's attackers. His bullets struck both the camel and the man's leg. The camel ran on several yards, but collapsed in a heap on the steaming desert floor. Its rider screamed as his wounded leg scraped along the sand, but he managed to pull himself away from the dying animal.

Said's pack camel had been running back and forth in a state of panic. The animal suddenly reared up and charged the injured man. It grabbed the Tuareg's robe at the shoulder with its teeth, pulled up, then flung the man back down. Using the hard pad of cartilage that protruded from its breastbone between its front legs, it battered the man to death.

In'Hout had been knocked down by the other warrior's

camel and had lost hold of his submachine gun. The Tuareg charged again and thrust forward with his spear. In'Hout jerked to one side at the last possible moment, reaching over with his right hand to grab the shaft of the weapon as it passed over his left shoulder. Getting a grip with both hands, he pulled it toward him with all the strength in his wiry body. The blue man started to topple but let go in time to keep his leg lock on his saddle. In'Hout fell backward onto the sand.

He was up in a second. The Tuareg drew his sword and turned his mount for another charge. Rather than wait for it, In'Hout ran straight for his attacker. Using the strong spear as a pole, he dug the point into the sand and vaulted upward, his feet catching the blue man in the chest and knocking him off of his animal.

In'Hout flew over the camel and tumbled on top of the Tuareg. He smashed the man in the face with both fists, grabbed for the fallen spear, stepped back, and ran the man through.

That left only one Tuareg. He and Said were standing face to face, the blue man with a sword and Said with his Reveilli rifle.

The Bedouin suddenly threw his weapon down and pulled a sword from the grasp of a dead Tuareg warrior. He waved Gideon and In'Hout away and turned to face his opponent.

The Tuareg lunged forward with a violent, high-pitched scream. Metal met metal, slicing the air. The Tuareg was the aggressor for the first moments. But Said suddenly faked right in an exaggerated motion, ducked down, and came in low to the left with a thrust. The man's parry was too slow to stop the forward motion of Said's blade, and the Tuareg warrior, a sword through his stomach, died with Allah's name on his lips.

Said coolly reached down to pick up his rifle, blew the sand off it, then cast his eyes at the carnage around him.

Gideon and In'Hout joined him, Gideon leading the pack camel by a rope.

"Should we round up their camels?" In'Hout asked.

The Bedouin looked at the Mehari trotters scattered about.

"No, let them go. We can follow them to find out if there's a Tuareg camp in the area. I would rather surprise any more warriors than have them surprise us."

Both men nodded. Said reached for a water flask and passed it among them. They greedily drank as they watched the camels slowly regroup, and head southwest.

"Let's go," Said said.

They walked across the torrid sands, the sun blistering hot. The only vegetation here was an occasional desert-thorn growing in the valleys between dunes, and in the still, seemingly lifeless desert, the only movement the men saw was a solo bustard gracefully riding the thermals above. During the first part of their trek, a hot arid breeze fanned their faces, but then it stopped, and the heat felt even more oppressive. Near midday, as they paused at the top of a dune, they saw in the distance what looked like a cool, shimmering lake.

Gideon pointed. "What in the world is—"

The Bedouin interrupted him with a laugh. "That's a mirage. On hot windless days, when one air layer is more dense than another, the light creates such illusions. The rays of light pass through the cool dense air, but bend upward on striking hot air, forming the magical lake before your eyes. It is Allah's way of testing our devotion to the desert, tempting us with the illusion of water."

They descended the steep windward slope of that dune and started up the more gradual leeward slope of another, several hundred yards behind the Mehari camels. On reaching the top, Said suddenly pitched down into the soft sand, and with a wave of his hand, signaled the others to stop. Leaving the pack camel behind, Gideon and In'Hout wormed their way up next to the guide, careful not to get sand in their Stens.

Below them in the next dune valley was the Tuareg camp, five huts of dried grass each about fifteen feet square and ten feet high. Nearby, three hobbled camels nibbled at scrubby camel thorn. The returning seven camels joined them. Three warriors, one with a rifle and two with swords and spears, hurried over to examine them.

Said, ducking back down behind the ridge of the dune,

shook his head in consternation. "I don't understand why the Tuareg would set up their *zeribas* here in this part of the desert where there is no water. I know why they chose this valley—there is more camel thorn here for the camels than in the other ones—but why make a camp on the edge of the Great Sand Sea nowhere near an oasis?"

"Do we take them?" Gideon asked, deferring to his guide.

"Yes. If we don't, they'll be on us in minutes. They'll follow the camel tracks back the other way to find out what happened to their tribesmen."

Gideon thought for a moment and then said, "I have a plan. We're out of effective range of the Stens. That means we have to depend on your rifle, Said. We'll spread out along the dune with you in the middle. In'Hout and I will distract them from the flanks while you pick them off. If you can, keep one of them alive for questioning. I want to know what they're doing here."

Gideon and In'Hout moved out in opposite directions. When they were equidistant from the Bedouin guide in the middle, they stopped and readied their weapons. Gideon waved the others forward.

They reached the top of the dune at the same time, hit the sand, and opened fire. Gideon, closest to a blue man, drew the first answering volley. Two bullets kicked up sand several feet from his right shoulder. But the warrior never got off a third shot, as Said blew away part of his torso.

One of the two remaining warriors ran toward the fallen Tuareg, while the other sprinted toward the huts. With three more shots, Said picked off the Tuareg running past him for his dwelling. That left one warrior. Gideon jumped up and rushed him, holding his fire. Said yelled down from the top of the dune in Arabic, telling the man to surrender.

Ignoring him, the Tuareg turned and flung his spear at Gideon. The American dodged the flying steel as the warrior bent to pick up the rifle lying in the sand.

Gideon heard the Reveilli fire twice. The Tuareg, hit in the chest and neck, fell onto the body of his tribesman.

Gideon ran forward to verify that all three Tuareg warriors were dead. He stood staring at the corpses in disappointment.

Said joined him. "None of them would have talked," he said simply. "That is their code."

The two walked toward the *zeribas*, then rushed inside, guns ready. In a moment, they had flushed out all the occupants. Cowering before their conquerors, their frightened eyes on the barrels of the guns, the prisoners emerged into the desert sun— five women, unveiled according to Tuareg custom; six children; and two slaves. All were dressed in long white shirts or in blue robes, and most were barefoot.

Gideon turned his attention to the two slaves. One was a tall black Nubian with tribal scars carved on his cheeks. The second was a young man with fine features, olive skin, and curly black hair.

Said spoke to them first in Arabic. No one replied.

Gideon tried a long shot. "Does anyone speak English?"

"I do," the young fine-featured man replied. "I speak your language."

Gideon couldn't quite place his accent. "Are you Egyptian?"

"No, Italian. My name is Tommaso Masucci."

Gideon's eyebrows rose. "Italian? How the hell did you end up as a slave to the Tuareg?"

The young man suddenly looked wary. "You are not British. Are you Australian?"

"I'm asking the questions," Gideon sharply retorted. "Now, what are you doing here?"

The young man ignored his question. "You couldn't be trying to trick me. You must be British or Anzac. If you were German, you wouldn't have fought the Tuareg."

"And why not?"

"Because the Tuareg are working for the Germans. The Germans asked them to come here."

"Why?" Gideon asked.

"To guard the desert. I—"

"Are there any more Tuareg in the area?" Said interrupted.

"Yes. Twelve of them. Some of their camels returned."

"What are they guarding?" Gideon demanded.

"I don't know. I don't even think the chieftain did. They were told they would be given gold and foodstuffs if they guarded the northern edge of the Great Sand Sea. They never went south of here."

"Why is it so important to you that we're not Germans?"

"I deserted from the Italian army," Masucci said.

"You'd better be telling us the truth," In'Hout warned him, narrowing his eyes. "Liars lose their tongues out here."

"It's true. I left the Italian army of my own free will. I swear it on the Virgin Mother—"

"But the Germans must have known you were Italian," In'Hout interrupted. "Why didn't they arrest you?"

"They didn't know. To them I was just a slave to the Tuareg. They thought I was an Arab. The Tuareg would never give away my identity. I am their property."

Said glanced toward the bodies of the dead warriors. "You *were* their property."

Masucci asked slyly, "Will you take me to Egypt?"

Gideon studied him. "Why did you leave the army?"

The young man met his eyes. "I wasn't afraid, it wasn't that."

"What then?"

Masucci took a deep breath, gathering his thoughts. "I came to Libya with my family three years ago. We settled in Zlithen, one of Mussolini's agricultural colonies. My father was chosen for this opportunity because he was a veteran of the Ethiopian campaign and a member of the National Fascist Party. Some opportunity." He paused and shook his head. "I embraced neither Fascism nor Mussolini's vision of a new Roman Africa. But I went along with my father's wishes, enlisting as soon as I came of age to fight the British. I was at the rout of Sidi Barrani last December and retreated in disgrace with the rest of the Italian army. I would have fought on as my father wished, but . . ." His voice trailed off.

"But what?" In'Hout asked impatiently.

"The Germans came to Africa and I learned the true meaning of Fascism." Rage flashed in the young man's dark eyes. "Nazi soldiers broke into our house, killed my father, then raped and killed my mother and sister."

"You saw this?" Gideon asked.

"No, I was in the field at Benghazi. But our neighbors saw the Germans leaving and informed me. It was then I decided to desert and join the fight against the Nazis and their pawns—even my fellow countrymen, if it came to that. I equipped myself and headed across the desert, only to be captured a month ago and held as a slave by the Tuareg."

Gideon stepped to one side and waved In'Hout and Said over to him.

"Quite a tale," he murmured. "It rings true, but it's also conceivable he's a plant placed here by the Germans."

"If so, he would not have been treated as a slave," Said offered. "I believe him."

Gideon turned toward the Dutchman. "Do you? Do we take him with us?"

In'Hout glanced over in the direction of the Italian. "If he's lying, he's a damn good actor. He could be an opportunist who will turn on us if the tide turns. But I'm willing to take him along."

"Settled, then." Gideon turned to Said. "What about the others?"

The Bedouin looked them over. "We'll send them on their way." He broke into a grin. "That is, unless either of you want a concubine for the afternoon. I'm sure the Tuareg women know how to make a man happy. Of course, you may wind up with a knife in your back."

"No woman is worth that much," In'Hout said in mock seriousness. "At least, I don't think so."

"I'll pass," Gideon agreed.

"Okay, we'll only take those camels we need. That will leave six for the women and children to return to Tuareg country. The Nubian can go with them. There is plenty of water for them and for us. The Germans must have trucked in those metal containers. We'll use one *zeriba* to camp in today, and they can dismantle the rest. We'll let them leave when darkness comes. Until then, one of us must be on watch."

"Fine," Gideon told him. "I'll leave it up to you and the Italian to deal with the Tuareg while In'Hout and I get some rest."

"You'll need it," the Bedouin said, gazing off to the south. "Tonight we cross the Great Sand Sea."

CHAPTER FIVE

MOUNTED ON MEHARI trotting camels, the pack dromedary trailing behind, the four men crossed the sandy dune-rippled plain. It was a crisp cold night. Glimmering stars against the huge ebony dome of sky illuminated their path.

Fuad El-Said's intended destination was an unmapped water hole in the area that the Bedouin considered the heart of the Great Sand Sea. The water was brackish and undrinkable there, but the Germans could treat it. It was worth a look.

From time to time as they traveled, Gideon checked his compass to verify their direction. Said used only the stars, his knowledge of local landforms, and his intuition to keep them on course.

The first sign of the Nazis—engines churning from the south—came about four a.m., when the men were about two hours from the targeted water hole.

"A convoy," Gideon said. "It must be."

They dismounted, hobbled their camels, and moved on foot toward the noise. Trudging through thick sand that shifted out from under them with each step, they climbed toward the top of a star dune. Finally, they reached the ridge and looked out over the valley. The moon had risen and they could make out the shapes that were slowly working their way across the desert floor.

"Look at the size of it!" In'Hout exclaimed.

There were twenty-four Opel and Daumier half-tracks, or

Maultiers, the German word for "mules," plus a half-dozen escort tanks stretched out in a long line moving southeast.

"What a stroke of luck," Gideon said with relish. "The convoy must be heading toward our mystery site."

"Or away from it," In'Hout pointed out.

"Do we follow it?" Said asked.

Gideon thought a moment. "I've got to take the chance and make contact here as Wolfgang Lichter. Even if the convoy is leaving the site, they'll have to make plans to get me delivered. You follow the convoy. If I'm sent off with an escort, you'll have to follow the tracks."

"In which case, let's hope the wind doesn't blow them away," the Bedouin guide said.

"What will you tell the krauts about the Bedouin who supposedly rescued you after the crash?" In'Hout asked.

"That they encountered the Tuareg and I took off on my own from the scene of battle. If the Germans should come across the Tuareg women, my story will hold up."

"I hope they buy it."

"I'm more worried about Lichter's fellow scientists, if there are any out here, than I am about convoy guards. After all, I do have Lichter's papers."

Gideon slid back down the dune to go for the documents in his saddlebag. The others followed. He handed Said his Sten gun.

"Are you taking a handgun, at least?" In'Hout asked.

"No, it's more likely the Bedouins wouldn't have let me carry one."

"Do you have a white cloth to wave as you approach the convoy? The guards will probably be trigger-happy."

Gideon opened and waved a handkerchief. "Keep an eye out. If my charade is discovered, I'll try to drop this behind. And if I don't get back to you within four days after I arrive at wherever the hell I'm going, return to Cairo. Radio Philaix in advance. You have the code?"

"Yes."

Gideon turned to Said. "How will I find you again?"

"Travel at night. Follow the north star. We'll camp on a

direct line with it and the site, as close as we deem it safe—probably two to three miles, but maybe more."

"Got it."

The Dutchman extended his hand. "Well, good luck then."

"*Allah yí sallimak.* May God protect you," the Bedouin said.

The Italian youth, Tommaso Masucci, stepped out of the shadows from where he had been watching. He took Gideon's hand and shook it firmly. "You're a brave man," he said.

Waving his white flag, Gideon descended, deliberately stumbling, toward the slow-moving convoy. He doubted he could be heard over the whine of the engines, but shouted for help in German anyway. He half expected a chattering burst of automatic fire as some guard took delight in dispatching what he might believe was a troublesome Bedouin.

A lookout riding on top of a tank in the middle of the convoy spotted Gideon first. His arm went up and the vehicles behind him stopped. The lumbering Panzer IV swung toward Gideon, its 75mm turret gun and its two 7.92mm machine guns ready to blast him to pieces. A light clicked on, blinding Gideon with its intense beam. He heard footsteps.

The searchlight clicked off. Ten men surrounded him with automatic weapons—Wehrmacht soldiers of the Afrika Korps, Gideon could make out by their insignia. A beefy *Oberleutnant* with thick features addressed him in German.

"Who are you? What are you doing here?"

"Thank God I've found you," Gideon said in Austrian-accented German. "My name is Wolfgang Lichter. I am an Austrian chemist. I was on my way to the Great Sand Sea in a Fieseler Storch when the plane crashed in a sandstorm. I would have died if the Bedouin hadn't found me."

Gideon handed his identification papers to the German officer.

The officer closely inspected the papers, then looked at Gideon appraisingly. "They gave you those clothes?" he finally asked.

"Yes," Gideon replied. "They saved my life, caring for

me when they came upon the wreck. They also brought me to the Great Sand Sea, as I asked."

"Then what are you doing here alone?"

"The Bedouins were attacked by another tribe yesterday—the Tuareg, they called them. The Tuareg were ferocious, and they were killing so many Bedouins that I took my first opportunity to slip away into the desert. I've been wandering all night. If I hadn't found you, I surely would have died. I ran out of water hours ago."

The *Oberleutnant* inspected the papers once again. "So you are going to the *Betonunterstand*? You have full clearance?"

Gideon drew himself up and let some irritation come into hs voice. "I am a scientist traveling on the personal orders of the Führer. I have suffered greatly, and I request that you see I am delivered to my destination as quickly as possible."

The tone and the mention of Hitler took the lieutenant back a bit. He handed Gideon his papers, saying "This convoy is headed for the *Betonunterstand*. You may ride along with us. When we arrive, the SS will verify your identity."

"They will reward you for taking me in, I assure you," Gideon said. "Now, if you would be so kind as to let me have some water?"

"Of course," the lieutenant said, his expression much more friendly. "I'll have a canteen brought to you." He hesitated a moment, then added, "Perhaps it is your clothing that occasions my suspicion. When I see you in a laboratory coat, I will have no more doubts."

"Yes, indeed," Gideon said. "I hope you will visit me at some future date."

The lieutenant bowed slightly, then led Gideon to a half-track. Gideon, breathing a quiet sigh of relief, eagerly climbed into the back and accepted a canteen.

He took a seat on the wooden bench of the personnel carrier. Surrounding him were the weatherbeaten soldiers of the Afrika Korps. The *Maultier*, its tracks clanking as they dug into the soft sand, moved out.

Most of the soldiers slept, their heads propped awkwardly against any surface that presented itself. But several of them eyed the newcomer in their midst. These troops weren't untested, Gideon could tell; they had the lean, confident look of well-seasoned soldiers. How many campaigns had they fought for Rommel? How much territory had they seized from the British, how many troops had they killed? Their presence as guards for this convoy testified to the importance of this *Betonunterstand*, or bunker, toward which they were headed.

Despite his curiosity, Gideon pretended to sleep, although he would not allow himself to drop off. He had already gauged the distance to the nearest machine pistol in case of trouble.

Dawn came. The convoy kept moving. The heat of the sun quickly penetrated the half-track's canvas covering. None of the soldiers slept now. They restlessly shifted about, trying to find a comfortable position in the cramped, broiling space. Gideon gazed out the back at the long line of trucks, wondering what they carried.

Finally, the convoy stopped. The trucks pulled up in pairs, the tanks spreading out to cover their flanks. The soldiers climbed out. Gideon followed, eyes searching the desert expectantly.

He saw only miles of sand—no sign of any kind of installation. The vast expanse of desert they had just traversed was a kind of plateau which dropped off dramatically to a lower plain, forming a sheer rock face about fifty feet high, brightly polished by wind and sand. The convoy had made a wide sweep around the west of this escarpment, where the ground sloped down gradually to the lower plain, and then angled back eastward to a point directly opposite the face of the long cliff.

Gideon noticed that this part of the Great Sand Sea was pure sand and rock, with no sign of life anywhere, not even scrub brush or camel thorn. Farther to the south, away from the escarpment, the sand seemed blackened, as if burned by the blazing sun. There were certainly no date palms to be seen in the area, the telltale sign of water near the surface.

And without water, how could there be a German facility here?

Suddenly, to Gideon's utter amazement, the rock face itself started to move. Giant doors, the same color and seemingly the same texture as the wind-scoured rock, slid open with a loud, grinding rumble.

The bunker, Gideon said to himself, built right into the escarpment. A perfect camouflage.

The *Oberleutnant* walked up to Gideon. "Come with me," he said.

He led Gideon over the sand toward the enormous doors, through which they passed into a gigantic antechamber carved out of rock and reinforced with massive ferroconcrete walls. Bare incandescent bulbs on the antechamber's seventy-foot-high ceiling cast yellow light below. Crates were stacked against the far wall, in the middle of which was another armored steel door apparently leading deeper into the rock. To the right, just inside the massive sliding doors, was a large steel tower, multileveled and open, leading all the way to the ceiling. There were eight guards on each of the four levels and two machine-gun nests. What looked like periscopes extended up from the tower's top level through the antechamber ceiling. To the left of the front doors, opposite the guard tower, was a second tower. This, however, was a solid platform on top of which were mounted four powerful 88 antiaircraft guns, pointing in different directions, as well as smaller caliber antipersonnel weapons and powerful beacons to sweep the skies. The ceiling directly over the 88s contained another pair of sliding doors. When the doors were opened, the guns could be raised upward on a giant hydraulic lift, for a formidable defense against an air attack on the bunker.

A *Hauptsturmführer* of the Waffen SS approached Gideon and the lieutenant from the lower level of the guard tower.

"Wer ist dies?" He was a small man with a pinched face and a brusque manner.

The Wehrmacht lieutenant answered for Gideon. "Wolfgang Lichter, an Austrian chemist. He says you're expecting him."

Gideon, smiling blandly, handed over the identification papers. The SS captain studied them carefully, going over them again and again.

Finally, the captain looked up. He spoke to the lieutenant first. "Yes, we are expecting him." Then he turned toward Gideon. "Where have you been?"

Gideon told the story of the crash and the Bedouin. The captain listened impassively and then, without saying a word, he turned and walked back to the tower. Gideon saw him inside the lower compartment making a telephone call. The captain stepped out again, carrying a clipboard, brushed past Gideon, and proceeded to oversee the unloading of the convoy.

Another man came through the bunker's inner door. He was wearing a white frock over civilian clothes—obviously a scientist.

Gideon tensed inside. This could be trouble. Any of the scientists might have been former colleagues of Lichter's and would recognize Gideon as a fraud.

The Phoenix leader scrutinized the scientist's face for any sudden reaction. Though powerfully built, the man looked tired and drawn. It was obvious that he had been working hard, as his eyes were red with bags beneath them, and the skin of his wide, chiseled face had a pallid cast.

A quick frown rippled across the man's brow—at the sight of either the Bedouin clothing or Gideon's face? —then disappeared quickly.

The man extended his hand. "Herr Lichter, my name is Semmeln Ulmer. I am delighted to see you. After all this time, both we and Berlin had given you up for lost. Whatever happened to you?"

"My Storch crashed in a sandstorm, and the pilot and the two guards were killed. As you can see by my clothing, I owe my life to the Bedouins. And to my good fortune in meeting up with the convoy."

"Well, it was a stroke of good fortune for the Third Reich. This project is of the highest importance, and we need you badly. I am a physicist, and our staff is strong in engineering. We have made great progress with the mechanical development.

But our most stubborn problems have been with the question of fuel. A chemist of your stature is exactly what we need."

Ulmer took Gideon's arm. "Come. Let's get you out of those clothes. You must be thirsty and hungry. And I want you to meet the rest of the scientific staff and see what we've accomplished here." He turned to the Wehrmacht officer who accompanied Gideon. "Thank you, lieutenant, for finding our chemist."

Ulmer led Gideon toward the inner doors along the far wall. They slid open along rollers, and the two men stepped into a long passageway.

They walked past concrete walls and metal doors. Ulmer identified some of the rooms as they passed them—the kitchen, the mess, washrooms, barracks. Gideon, stunned at the size of the facility, counted twelve rooms in all, plus another pair of sliding doors at the end of the long hall.

Ulmer stopped at room number nine. He flicked on a light switch and showed Gideon inside. Functional metal-framed beds and lockers lined the concrete walls. Gideon noticed vents in the ceiling—the air supply, evidently from shafts leading to the surface.

"Our quarters are not plush, but they are functional. It is a sacrifice we make for the greater glory of the Fatherland."

"I understand," Gideon said. He gazed around him, then asked, "What do you do for water here? I saw no sign of an oasis."

"We have tapped what the Arabs call the *behar tahtani*, the 'sea of the underworld.' We draw our water from deep wells drilled hundreds of meters down through the rock."

"Exactly how far?"

"Three hundred and fifty meters from the lower level," Ulmer said proudly. He walked to a locker, opened it, and tossed Gideon a set of clothing. "Here, these should fit you. You can change in the washroom. Here's a toilet kit."

Gideon took the small leather bag and followed Ulmer back out to the hall and down to the washroom door.

"Take your time," Ulmer said. "I'll be waiting for you in room twelve."

Gideon entered the stark, institutional washroom. Out here in the desert, however, the facility seemed like sheer luxury. He took a quick shower, shaved, donned the change of clothing, then rejoined Ulmer.

"Would you like something to eat before we go below? A bite to hold you until lunch?" the physicist asked.

"No, I'll wait. I'm anxious to see the rest of the facility."

They moved to the sliding doors at the end of the passageway. Ulmer pressed a button mounted on the wall, and the doors slid open. They stepped on to an elevator. An armed guard was at the controls, a Waffen SS private.

The elevator car dropped down the vertical shaft, then glided to a halt. The doors opened, and Ulmer and Gideon stepped out into another, broader passageway that ran directly below the upper one. This one was very long, and Gideon calculated it led out beyond the face of the escarpment to a point beneath the desert floor.

Ulmer explained the layout as they passed more doors on this level—the generator room, the well room, machine shops, and various laboratories. He poked his head into the labs, rounding up members of the staff to introduce to Gideon. With each new face and handshake, Gideon flinched inside at the possibility that the man knew the real Wolfgang Lichter. But it seemed no one knew Lichter personally—only by reputation.

Ulmer and Gideon continued down the long passageway, their footsteps echoing on the cement floor, and headed for one more set of sliding armored steel doors, where eight Waffen SS guards were stationed.

This is it, Gideon told himself. I'll finally discover the purpose behind the building of this incredible complex.

Ulmer pushed a button. The doors slid open, and they stepped through.

Gideon looked upward in open-mouth astonishment. In the middle of an immense vault, standing upright, was a long sleek aircraft, the likes of which Gideon had never seen. Coming to a streamline point, it looked like a huge artillery shell, with four stabilizing fins and massive jet engines at its base.

Nazi Germany was at the point of unleashing the most awesome weapon in the history of warfare—a jet-propelled, long-range rocket. This was, Gideon realized suddenly, his most important mission of the war. As he gaped at the enormous weapon, horror ran through him like an electric current.

CHAPTER SIX

GIDEON LAY FLAT on his back, gazing upward into the darkness. Around him in the small room, three other scientists breathed heavily in deep sleep. Although Gideon hadn't slept for thirty-six hours, he was unable to drop off.

The day had been immensely trying, far worse than the strain of battle. Both undercover work and fighting required a finely tuned intuitive sense—*Fingerspitzengefühl*, as the Germans called it, literally "intuition in the fingers." Both required intense concentration. But battle was a kind of letting go, while the other involved a rigid self-discipline—concealing the real Scott Gideon while concentrating on creating the identity of an Austrian.

The charade had worked so far. The only tense moment came when a Hungarian engineer had held back his hand on being introduced, his eyes surprised and suspicious. Gideon had felt the adrenaline pumping through him, and it was all he could do to resist scanning the room for a weapon.

Then the man, Tibor Horvath, had given Gideon a firm handshake. The Phoenix leader relaxed slightly and followed Semmeln Ulmer on the rest of the tour. But he made a mental note to be wary in Horvath's presence in the future.

The rest of the scientific staff had welcomed "Lichter" effusively. In his briefing by the heads of the departments, he learned why.

The *Betonunterstand* had been built the year before, after an agreement had been reached between Hitler and Mussolini.

Indeed, Gideon was told, it was one of the main reasons the Germans had come to Italy's aid in Libya. Other work was being done on a short-range "A-series" rocket at European sites. But the vastness of the desert was necessary for testing the deadly "XX-series" rockets that could reach any point in England from German soil. The projected range of the weapons might mean American cities could be reached, should England fall.

In his briefings, Gideon was told a breakthrough was near. Almost all the structural problems had been worked out; the two remaining serious difficulties were both chemistry-related. The first had to do with bifuels, a combination of fuels that would produce the tremendous sustained power necessary to propel the rocket on a thousand-mile flight. Liquid hydrogen and alcohol combinations had proved unsatisfactory on test flights. The hope for future launches was a combination of sulfuric acid and hydrogen.

The second problem concerned the type of explosive to be delivered. Amatol, a mixture of TNT and ammonium nitrate, stayed stable at supersonic speeds, but it didn't cause the explosive force the Germans sought. To date, more powerful mixtures had prematurely detonated from the intense heat caused by the friction of the atmosphere on the metal casing of the warhead. This latter problem was the reason for calling in Lichter, an expert in the chemistry of volatile substances.

The chemical problems had been the sole topic of conversation during and after the evening meal. Gideon knew enough to hold up his end of general conversations. The chemistry of explosives had been his main area of interest during his studies at the University of Brussels before the war. For the time being, the others accepted his expressed reluctance to offer more detailed suggestions without further study of the previous test results.

He knew he couldn't stall for long, as Ulmer would want Lichter's work to begin immediately.

It was possible he might use his access to explosives to carry out an act of sabotage. But that would only slow down the work for a few days or weeks rather than destroy the

Betonunterstand. He had to put a permanent end to the development of the awesome weapon that could mean total German victory. But how?

First, Gideon thought, he must learn all he could about the rocket facility. Then he had to escape from the bunker, a dangerous mission in itself. Elite Waffen SS guards were everywhere. Even now he could hear four guards walking the long passageway outside his door. Eight guards were posted at the one door to the launch vault where the towering rocket stood, and pairs of soldiers guarded every other point of egress. In addition, an SS storm trooper was assigned to accompany every scientist throughout the complex both day and evening.

And if he did reach the desert and avoid being picked up by patrols, what then? The underground bunker was virtually invulnerable to air attack. The German patrols were so extensive, a major ground assault force couldn't get within a hundred miles without being chewed up by superior Luftwaffe and Italian air force attacks.

The only answer was a commando raid by the Phoenix team, entering the bunker somehow under cover of darkness and planting explosives.

As he lay exhausted in the darkness, the obstacles seemed insurmountable. Finally, he drifted off into uneasy sleep, his dreams filled with images of death and destruction.

The next morning, Gideon sat at a small desk, reviewing folders of technical reports. He'd been awakened at five a.m., and somehow he'd dragged his weary body out of bed. During breakfast, Semmeln Ulmer told him he'd have a day to brief himself on the progress of the research before going into the laboratory. Gideon smiled inwardly when told he should take time to thoroughly familiarize himself with the facility as well.

After a moment's hesitation, Gideon decided to take the risk of mentioning that he found the constant companionship of the Waffen SS guard distracting. The project director assured him not to take the surveillance personally. Orders had come directly from Berlin to take all precautions against sabotage by or against scientists. Only Ulmer himself had free access.

After breakfast, Gideon was joined by his guard. Although the *Sturmmann* couldn't have been more than twenty or twenty-one, he had the cold, confident arrogance of a high-ranking officer. He was tall and blond, with the Aryan square-boned features so prized by the Waffen SS "supermen." He treated the supposed Herr Lichter with disdain, as an inferior Austrian, even though the scientist held a vastly more prestigious position. He never took his eyes off Gideon, and he kept his machine pistol at the ready.

Gideon knew he had little chance of establishing any rapport with Corporal Kreutz that might prove advantageous. He decided to go in the other direction, building the Nazi's disdain into a hatred that might cloud his judgment.

Gideon stretched, then got up from his desk. He waved at the corporal as if he were a servant. "Come along, Kreutz," he called out. "You look like you're falling asleep on your feet. I think you need a walk, so follow me."

Gideon started for the door, noting with pleasure that the German's jaw had tightened. "I know you're tired," he called out over his shoulder, "but try not to bump into anything, like a good boy."

The Nazi grunted in disgust as Gideon led the way down the long lower passageway. He stopped first at a high room where sheet metal was bent to form the rocket frame. He continued past the heavy machinery to the workrooms where the critical guidance components were constructed, through machine shops, and then into the large assembly room where the rockets were welded together. From there, the rockets were rolled on tracks through wide sliding doors down a second lower passageway to the launch vault. The only other door in this passageway was the entrance to the vaults containing the rocket-fuel storage tanks.

Gideon, taking his time, asked numerous questions while he memorized the location of guard posts, alarm systems, doorways, and ventilation shafts. He was in an engineering section when he suddenly realized he was being scrutinized intently by someone other than the Waffen SS guard.

It was Tibor Horvath, the thickset Hungarian who had acted so strange on their first meeting. Horvath had turned away from the workers he was supervising to stare at Gideon.

Warily, Gideon started on to the next shop. But the Hungarian summoned Gideon over. He hesitated, then thought to himself that if the confrontation had to come sometime, it might as well come now.

Gideon joined the engineer, who took him by the arm and led him to a drawing board where a set of plans were laid out. Gideon glanced to one side and saw that Kreutz had joined the Hungarian's SS guard; they stood talking just out of earshot.

Horvath raised his hand to point at the plans, but his words were about an entirely different subject.

"I know you are not Wolfgang Lichter," he said in German. "I knew Lichter when I was studying in Austria. That means you are a spy. The British found his body in the desert and sent you in his place, correct?"

Gideon hesitated, trying to think clearly through his shock. Then he asked, "Why didn't you expose me when we first met?"

"I'm a scientist, not a barbarian," the Hungarian replied. He lowered his voice and advised, "Ask a scientific question."

Gideon took the warning. He asked about tests concerning the thickness of the warhead's casing. As Horvath replied, Gideon noticed his SS guard strolling past, eyes and ears open.

They kept the discussion on scientific terms for a few moments more. When Kreutz was out of range again, the Hungarian said, "I'm here against my will. I despise the Nazis and I hate to work on this immoral project. I've wanted to escape for a long time. You must be planning to leave here. When you go, I must go with you."

Gideon stared into the eyes of the engineer. There was always the chance this was a trap, an attempt to uncover the purpose of his mission before he was arrested and shot.

But he didn't think so. Gideon's ability to judge men

instantaneously had kept him alive in enemy territory for years, and the Hungarian struck Gideon as sincere.

"I'll help you get to freedom," Gideon said. "But you have to do one thing for me."

"Anything."

"I want you to help me destroy the *Betonunterstand*."

The Hungarian gazed slowly around the shop in disbelief. "But . . . how? This place is immense, and we are only two."

"I have friends," Gideon said. "I'm going to rendezvous in the desert with . . ."

His voice trailed off as he heard a call for attention behind him. Gideon turned to see that Semmeln Ulmer had come into the shop. The director of the research facility was beaming.

"I have good news," Ulmer said. "Through hard work, we have been able to advance the next test flight to tomorrow after sunset."

The staff broke into applause.

Ulmer came over to Gideon. "Herr Lichter," he said, "this change in the schedule is most fortunate for you. You will be able to observe for yourself our problems with the fuel and payload. You must prepare carefully."

"I certainly will, Herr Direcktor," Gideon stated. He turned back to the Hungarian and said, "You have been most informative. Perhaps we can continue our discussion about the warhead design at lunch."

The Hungarian bowed slightly. Then Gideon followed Ulmer from the shop.

The dining room buzzed with talk of the test flight. Gideon, delayed by a conversation with the director, was disappointed to see Horvath sitting at a full table. Reluctantly, he sat with another group of scientists.

Again the scientists tried to draw out his opinions about propellants and the stability of explosives. And again, Gideon said as little as possible, playing the taciturn, cautious scientist. From the sophistication of the questions thrown at him, Gideon realized more and more that his role could have only a short run.

He was still eating when he saw Horvath prepare to leave. Hurriedly, Gideon excused himself and followed. He reached the Hungarian as he waited for the elevator.

"I was anxious to talk with you again," Gideon said.

He saw Horvath's eyes flicker. Gideon turned slightly to spy Kreutz, his unshakable shadow.

"Those equations for computing rocket-skin temperature for different angles of trajectory," Gideon said, "should prove quite useful to my work. Lowering the temperature just a few degrees may lead to an exponential rather than arithmetic increase in payload."

"Interesting," Horvath said.

The doors opened, and they stepped into the large car. Although they were the only passengers, Kreutz stood at Gideon's shoulder.

Gideon gave the SS guard a look of deep annoyance. He said to Horvath, "The good corporal here can't bear to miss a technical conversation. I understand he wants to add a degree in rocketry to his already legendary skill at bayoneting babies."

Horvath's mouth dropped open in astonishment. Out of the corner of his eye, Gideon could see the rage on Kreutz's face.

"How dare you talk to a member of the Waffen SS like that?" the corporal snarled.

Gideon turned to him, his face registering anger and contempt. "Swine," Gideon said. "I have been sent here on personal order of the Führer to complete work that will ensure the triumph of the Third Reich. I will not be treated like a criminal by a thug."

Gideon turned to Horvath, adding, "If it weren't for the war, our blond-haired boy here would no doubt be mopping swill off beerhall floors."

Gideon sensed that the SS guard was on the verge of completely losing his composure, when the elevator came to a halt and the doors opened.

"I am reporting you to my lieutenant," Kreutz said. "You will not move from this spot."

The SS corporal stormed down the hall to a black phone hanging from the wall.

"Now you've done it," Horvath said to Gideon in an anxious voice. "You've exposed yourself, and—"

Gideon grabbed him, cutting him off in mid-sentence. "Don't worry about me. Listen carefully. Ten days from now, a week from Friday, I have to leave the bunker and then get back inside the bunker during the middle of the night—with other men."

Horvath's face registered confusion. "Other men? How? The doors are locked and the controls heavily guarded."

"The ventilation shafts go to the surface, don't they?"

"Yes," Horvath replied. "But at the bottom are huge fans made from airplane propellers. You would be cut to ribbons."

Gideon thought for a moment, then asked, "Do the motors driving the fans ever fail?"

"Occasionally. Sand blows inside and . . ." Horvath's voice trailed off as a look of comprehension dawned on his face. "Ah, I understand. You want me to arrange for a motor to fail?"

"Yes. The ventilation shaft in the wall between the kitchen and the mess hall. At three a.m. Can you do it?"

Horvath paused in obvious confusion. "I don't know," he finally answered. "There are guards patrolling constantly."

Gideon put a hand on his arm. "If you do, it will be the end of the *Betonunterstand* and the XX rocket. It's our only chance."

Horvath heard the sound of jackboots, and his face registered resolve.

"Do it," Gideon whispered. "Find a way and do it."

CHAPTER SEVEN

THE COUNTDOWN BEGAN at noon. The level of activity in the bunker increased dramatically as the hours passed. With most of the scientists busy with the frenetic preparations, Gideon found himself free to inspect in more detail the bunker's facilities and defenses. As launch time neared, he returned to his lab to commit the most important details to paper.

He'd been working for over half an hour when the door opened, and Semmeln Ulmer walked in.

"I've been looking for you, Lichter," Ulmer said.

"You've found me," Gideon replied.

Ulmer's expression was serious. He sat in the chair across from Gideon's desk and said, "I had a long conversation with Colonel Steg about you this morning. He considers the insult to his man a matter of—"

"I don't care what the SS thinks of me," Gideon interrupted. "I'm sure you're aware, if the colonel isn't, that I was sent here under orders issued by the Führer himself. My assignment is to assist in the completion of a project that will ensure the final and total victory of the Third Reich. If Colonel Steg is unhappy with the way I talk to his corporal, I suggest that he pass his complaints on to Berlin. I'm sure they'll be sympathetic."

Gideon's withering sarcasm took the wind out of Ulmer's sails. He hesitated for a moment, seemingly at a loss for words. Then he managed to say, "I know why you're here.

Still, this facility is under the command of the SS, and we must observe—"

"I must make that rocket work," Gideon interjected again. "That is what the Führer has assigned me to do and that is what I will do. If I am not allowed to work without harassment, then I will contact Berlin."

Ulmer was thin-lipped and silent.

Gideon sat for a moment, then said in a more conciliatory tone, "I don't mean to make things difficult for you, Ulmer. You must forgive my temper. But after the horror of the plane crash and those awful days in the desert with those barbarians, I am exhausted. Yet what do I find? I'm ready to offer my services as a scientist to the greater glory of our Fatherland, but instead, I'm treated as a common criminal by some idiot solider."

Ulmer appeared grateful at the turn in the conversation. "I'm so sorry. Both the colonel and I did forget your ordeal. And no doubt this corporal was too zealous. You do recognize the need for security, though, do you not, Lichter?"

Gideon smiled. "Of course I do. And I will tolerate this man's presence. As long as he does not interfere in the work I have been sent here to do."

"I will see that he does not," Ulmer said. He got to his feet. "I am going up to the escarpment to watch the test flight. Will you join me?"

Gideon bit his lip in thought. "The control room has observation ports?"

"Through periscopes," Ulmer said, "so the observers are not blinded. Once the rocket is airborne, you can go into the launch vault, but the angle of vision through the doors above is limited."

"I understand," Gideon said. "But from the control room, I can see the ignition and initial thrust of the propulsion system. I think that would be valuable for my work."

"Of course," Ulmer replied. "And you'll be perfectly safe in the control room. Its protection was put to the test when a rocket exploded in the launch vault four months ago. I myself was in the control room and felt not a thing."

"Excellent," Gideon said, rising to his feet and extending his hand. "To a good flight."

The launch vault was at the extreme southern end of the underground bunker. The control room was a pillbox between two sets of doors on the north wall. The huge doors through which the rockets passed from the assembly room made up one set. The doors to the main eastern passageway were the only other entrance into the launch vault as far as Gideon knew.

The loudspeaker announced twenty minutes to launch as Gideon walked out of the laboratory into the east corridor followed by Corporal Kreutz. Gideon moved south, keeping to the side to avoid the technicians and soldiers hurrying to catch the elevators to the upper levels of the bunker complex.

Since the moment Ulmer announced the test, Gideon had concentrated on taking advantage of his best opportunity to escape. He had discarded the plan to join Ulmer and the others on the escarpment, which was outside the bunker, since it would be difficult to slip away without being noticed. And unless In'Hout and Said were within an hour's march of the bunker—an unlikely contingency—he'd certainly be discovered by the massive search his disappearance would cause.

The loudspeaker announced eighteen minutes to blast off. Gideon stopped for a moment to let a guard squad pass. Then he moved down to the door to the launch vault and pressed the switch that opened the electronically controlled barriers.

Kreutz was at his side. "Access to the launch vault is forbidden within thirty minutes of launch," the corporal said sharply.

Gideon ignored him, and when the passage cleared, he stepped inside the vault and hit the switch that electronically closed the door. Kreutz, at his heels, was almost caught when the door slammed shut.

The vault was black, the lights having been sealed off in preparation for the blast. A rumbling noise came from above, and the thick steel doors that formed the ceiling of the vault fifty meters above rolled open, revealing the desert sky. In the dimming light of dusk, Gideon could make out the sleek, lethal-looking lines of the huge XX rocket.

Gideon stared at the rocket a moment. Then he took a deep breath to relax himself and called out, "Kreutz."

The SS soldier approached. He said, "We have to get out of—"

Gideon suddenly kicked upward, catching the German in the groin. Kreutz doubled over, his machine pistol clattering on the concrete floor. Gideon clasped his hands together and slammed them down on the back of the SS guard's neck, dropping him to his knees. Gideon launched another kick, but the German managed to avoid the attack by rolling to the left.

Gideon plunged on him. Kreutz got his massive right hand firmly around Gideon's throat. Desperate for air, Gideon chopped down with the side of his hand, snapping Kreutz's wrist. Gideon then smashed the heel of his hand into the Nazi's nose, driving the bone into the skull. Blood poured from Kreutz's eyes as he fell back, dead.

Gideon leaped to his feet, listening for the sound of jackboots. All he heard was the hissing of gases from the pressure valve on the rocket's propellant chamber. Then he faintly heard the loudspeaker in the corridor outside announce fourteen minutes to launch.

Gideon glanced upward. The rocket seemed suddenly alive, like a powerful god glaring down at him.

Gideon knew he had to get out of there fast. He grabbed Kreutz's body and dragged it south, to be sure he could not be seen by the periscopes in the control room. Hurriedly, he stripped the Waffen SS uniform off the body and put it on. He dressed Kreutz in his civilian clothes, hoping the Nazis would believe him to be Lichter.

Gideon was gambling that the Germans would believe his baiting had finally ignited the temper of the SS corporal. When the incinerated body was found after the blast, Gideon prayed that they'd assume Kreutz had killed Lichter and fled the bunker. He doubted they'd launch an all-out search, as the relentless desert could be counted on to be judge and executioner.

Gideon finished with the body. The SS uniform was too big in the shoulders, but otherwise fit well enough. Gideon slung the MP40 over his shoulder, returned to the door to the corridor, and pushed the switch.

Nothing happened. Gideon hit the switch twice more, with the same lack of result. Then he remembered the launch-sequence plan he'd reviewed—electricity to the doors was to be cut off ten minutes before blast-off to prevent accidental opening.

Gideon broke into a run, circling the rocket away from the control room. He knew there were no interior controls for the huge doors into the assembly rooms. His only hope was to find some other way out of the vault.

But that, too, was locked. As he uselessly circled the pad, he heard the loudspeaker announce eight minutes to launch. He swore, slumping against the pad in frustration. Above, there was a fiery tint to the sky as the sun dipped below the horizon. It seemed to Gideon a gloomy prediction of his own fiery end, and he looked away.

Then he spotted it—a round steel grate in the northeast corner of the vault. Gideon dropped to the floor to stay out of sight of the control room and crawled toward what must serve as a drainage system for the vault. He grabbed the grate and pulled. It didn't budge. He used the barrel of the MP40 as a crowbar. At first, the grate resisted. Then, with a creak that echoed loudly throughout the launch vault, it began to move on its hinge.

Gideon couldn't see into the darkness below, but he didn't have time to worry about it. He lowered himself into the opening, holding onto the edge until he was suspended in the blackness. Then he let go.

The drop was only a few feet. He hit and tumbled to his left, smacking his elbow into a slimy stone wall.

He still couldn't see anything. In his mind, he ran quickly through the layout of the bunker. The elevator ran to the upper levels from the north end of the corridor, but it would be shut down now. Most bulk materials were lowered by crane from the opening at the top of the launch vault, a crane that had been rolled well away from the opening in preparation for the test. Off the east corridor was a smaller vertical shaft with a metal ladder that could be used by personnel in the event a power failure should make the elevators inoperable.

Gideon knew he was now safe from the blast. But the prospect of being captured and tortured by the Nazis if he failed to escape wasn't much more comforting. That smaller vertical shaft was his only chance, if he could get to it from where he was.

He took off to his right, using the stone wall as guidance. In twenty meters, he came to a junction, and took a ninety-degree turn to the right. A surge of hope went through him. Ahead, he could see a ray of light through the gloom.

He broke into a run. As hoped, the drainage system did indeed run into the vertical shaft, but the end of the tunnel was blocked by a locked door of iron bars. Gideon instantly decided he had to gamble all. He fired two bullets from the machine pistol, shattering the padlock, and quickly began to climb.

The bars were slippery, and it was all he could do to hang on. When he reached the locked door to the lower level, he heard the loudspeaker announce five minutes to launch. He climbed faster.

The top of the vertical shaft came to a riveted steel trapdoor that opened into the antechamber, the first area Gideon had seen when he'd entered the bunker. He had no choice but to hope that with the launch so near, he could slip out the door unchallenged.

He reached the top, took a moment to get his breath, then pushed.

The trapdoor opened a crack and Gideon peered out. There were lanterns spread around the huge high-ceilinged antechamber to supply light while the power was out for the launch. Waffen SS troops were all about, some posted, others climbing the two towers to the doors opening onto the escarpment. The big sliding doors leading to the desert were closed.

The trapdoor was against the exit, near the wall behind the gun tower. The guards at the machine-gun nests on the opposite tower would surely see Gideon emerging.

With a confident, deliberate motion, Gideon pushed the door completely open and pulled himself up. Then, crouching, he closed the trapdoor behind him and stood.

No one seemed to be paying any attention to him. Gideon breathed a quick sigh of relief, then turned his mind to his next move—he had less than three minutes to go.

The electric lifts had raised the antiaircraft guns to the escarpment, probably in case enemy planes spotted the rocket in flight. Since the gun tower was the closer of the two, Gideon headed for it. Either route he chose, he would have to walk close to SS troops.

He fell in behind another solider and followed him up the narrow metal staircase. He reached the top unchallenged, then began to climb the extension ladder to the top of the gun platform.

When he surfaced, he found himself in the middle of a circle of antiaircraft guns, the biggest of which were the deadly 88s. Surrounding the guns, beacons were pointed upward at the sky. Members of the gunnery crews rushed to their positions around Gideon.

He stopped to take a deep breath of fresh air. The sight of the open sky above renewed his energy, even if he still was far from free.

"Two minutes to launch," the loudspeaker boomed in German.

Gideon crossed to the far side of the platform, then stepped out onto the sand-covered rock that formed the natural surface of the escarpment. From this angle, looking out over the lower plain where the launch vault's doors had been opened, he could just discern the narrow nose of the XX rocket. Most of the observers stood a hundred yards back from the edge, wearing their protective goggles.

Gideon glanced at his watch. A little more than one minute. He had to pass directly before the scientists and senior SS staff to get to the northern edge of the escarpment, from where he had to make his escape.

He'd have to brazen it out. But he needed a pair of protective goggles to help conceal his face.

Noticing a pair strung from the sight of a gun, he dashed over, grabbed them, and secured them around his head.

"Einen Augenblick. Das tut man nicht!" the gunner yelled at him.

Gideon ignored him, walking quickly away. Fortunately, the artilleryman couldn't leave his post so close to blast-off.

Gideon neared the spectators. As he walked, he spotted the metal hoods and wire mesh that marked the tops of the three ventilation shafts that rose to the escarpment. The hoods had been painted brown and covered with sand to disguise their location from the air. Gideon stopped for a moment to fix the site of the shafts in his mind.

Then he resumed walking, pressing the helmet lower on his forehead. Most of the scientists were in his path. Gideon walked more briskly, as if carrying out an urgent order.

One thought soothed him—if he was discovered, he could kill a large number of the scientists with the MP40 before he went down. That would at least slow the XX project.

The fact that launch time was within seconds worked to Gideon's advantage. The spectators were staring at the space beyond the ledge, anticipating the rocket that would roar by.

Gideon slipped past the first of the group. A man on his left—no one he recognized—glanced his way, his eyes hidden behind the dark goggles, then looked back toward the lower plain. Gideon bumped into two men to his right, but they were busy talking about the target for this flight—a dune eighteen miles to the south—and they didn't turn.

Gideon spotted Semmeln Ulmer about twenty paces forward, standing with two high-ranking officers. The director stood perfectly still, eyes riveted southward in intense expectancy.

Then, directly in front of him, Gideon saw Tibor Horvath. The Hungarian turned toward him. From the way his body stiffened, Horvath obviously recognized him. If the engineer had cold feet about cooperating with Gideon, this would be the perfect time to raise an alarm.

But Horvath turned his head back toward the plain. Gideon reached the rear of the spectators and turned around as if to watch. Everyone seemed to be frozen in place. Nearly a month of hard work since the last test was culminating in this moment.

At that moment, there came a thunderous roar and a brilliant flash of light from the inside of the vault. The XX rocket shot upward, a huge missile of steel with a fountain of fire trailing behind. There was an earsplitting boom and a jagged ball of dark orange-black flames seared the sky. The XX rocket had exploded just as it began its climb.

Gideon scrambled up the ridge of sand and leaped. He landed on the downslope, then rolled to the bottom.

In the stillness of the desert evening, he could hear the Germans shouting. Gideon flattened himself against the sand, waiting for the beam of light sweeping the darkness, for the click of cartridges being chambered, for the sound of soldiers shuffling through the sand.

He waited and waited, ticking off the endless seconds in his mind. Gradually, the sounds on the other side of the ridge faded away, and Gideon rolled onto his back. After a moment or two, he spotted his compass—Polaris, the north star.

He stood up and started to run into the coolness of the night.

CHAPTER EIGHT

A MAGAZINE CLICKED into place. The sound of the bolt being cocked followed. Gideon caught a flash of the barrel's blue steel glistening in the moonlight.

Then a voice spoke in broken German. "Take one more step and I'll blow your Nazi face off."

"You'd shoot up this lovely mug?" Gideon called out in English.

"Gideon!" In'Hout exclaimed. "At the sight of that kraut's uniform, I almost opened up." He laughed. "Shit, would I have been in the doghouse with Philaix!"

They hugged in greeting. Fuad El-Said emerged from the black tent and also gave Gideon a welcoming embrace. Tommaso Masucci followed behind him. "You made it!" he exclaimed.

"Yes, I made it. Just barely. Two days of deception, a hairsbreadth escape, and a long desert hike, but here I am. I can hardly believe it myself. I was beginning to think I missed the camp."

"Any chance you were followed?" In'Hout asked.

"No, I've been checking constantly. But there's a good chance a team will be sent out in the morning if my ruse is discovered."

"We'll leave at once," the Bedouin said. "We'll wipe out our tracks behind us and hope that the wind will pick up enough tonight to blow away all traces leading up to here. I shall—"

"Okay then, it's settled," In'Hout interrupted. "But before anything else, tell us what the hell we saw shooting up into the sky and exploding."

Gideon looked from one man to the other. They awaited his answer with a mixture of dread and fascination.

"That, my friends, was a prototype rocket—the XX—a self-propelled aircraft that will be able to fly without pilots and carry out bombing attacks from great distances. Unless, of course, we stop it."

In'Hout shook his head. "My God, rockets now. Nothing like German ingenuity when it comes to killing."

Said's eyes were wide. For once his placid demeanor dissolved and he seemed truly shaken.

"And how do we stop it?" he asked.

"Did you see the bunker when you were following the convoy?"

"From a distance. When the trucks stopped, we swung around to the south. From the top of a dune we were able to make out with field glasses an opening in the rock face. But that was all. We didn't dare move any closer."

"So we circled north to camp," In'Hout added. "It was remarkable enough you got in, much less that you got out again."

Gideon smiled. "Yankee ingenuity," he said. "And it's going to take a hell of a lot more of it to destroy the bunker."

"How are we going to do it?" In'Hout asked.

"I'm going to radio Philaix to send in the rest of Phoenix. I have a man inside, a Hungarian, who will help us enter the complex. All we have to do is elude a battalion of Waffen SS."

In'Hout grinned. "We've done it before. We'll do it this time."

"Right," Gideon said. He turned to Said. "We have to choose a good place for the parachute drop, somewhere near our hiding spot."

The Bedouin scanned the nighttime horizon. "It has to be due north of here. To the west, we risk running into other convoys. To the east, toward Egypt, the Germans constantly patrol by air."

"Okay," Gideon said. "And one more thing. How about a change of Bedouin clothing? I think this SS uniform has served its purpose for now."

"In the tent," Said replied.

They broke camp, loading their gear onto the camels. Said rigged up a blanket, weighted with his rifle, to drag behind a camel and wipe away their tracks.

They set off northward into the night. The bobbing, swaying motion of the camel worked on Gideon's fatigue. He was too exhausted to combat the lulling effect, but he held tightly to the Tuareg saddle as he dropped into a half-sleep.

Just before dawn they reached a wide expanse of duneless soft sand about sixteen miles north of the *Betonunterstand*, an ideal location for a drop. They decided not to set up the camp immediately. If planes were sent to scout for the missing man, they would easily sight the black Bedouin tent. Said went to hobble the camels several miles away in an area of camel thorn. At the camp the supplies and gear were camouflaged under burlap sacks. The men would spend daylight hours under the sacks, sleeping if they could.

Gideon set about drawing up and transcribing the message to be radioed to Philaix in code. First, he wanted to bring in the other Phoenix members—Avrahm Brusilov, Marcel Charvey, Oscar Kinelly, and Eliska Dobrensky. Each would be armed for close combat with knives, pistols, grenades, and submachine guns—British Stens were ideal for fighting in enemy territory, since they used the same 9mm ammunition as the German MP40. They'd also need desert survival packs containing maps, compasses, canteens, food rations, and desert hats for protection from the sun. To get down inside the bunker, they'd need flashlights, a wire cutter, a grappling hook, and sufficient wire-cord rope.

Next, Gideon turned his attention to the problem of the explosives. He had decided to destroy the bunker by detonating the 25,000 gallons of rocket fuel stored in five huge tanks in vaults on the lower level. Plastic explosives would blow huge holes in the tanks, but to be sure the vapors ignited,

Gideon wanted an incendiary in the explosives mixture. Thermite mixed with a bit of oil would do the trick.

Packaging was a problem, however. They had to place charges in at least a half-dozen spots on each fuel tank. In addition, Gideon wanted to detonate the 55-gallon barrels of highly volatile chemicals used as fuel additives, and tying those charges to the tanks would take time.

Then the solution came to Gideon—limpet mines designed to be planted on the hulls of ships. The mines contained three pounds of plastic explosives in a magnetic half-moon casing. He'd order them with simple clock fuses that could be set to explode on any delay from one minute to four hours. Gideon decided to order three times the minimum he'd thought they'd need. Although he didn't like to think that some of the team could be killed before they reached the fuel tanks, he had to plan for the possibility.

Gideon estimated that Philaix would probably need a week to fly the rest of the team in from England and assemble the supplies. He encoded the information that he would light flares at the landing sight every morning at two a.m., beginning six days from now.

The attack would begin at three a.m. on the tenth day, and they should be out of the bunker in an hour. If they were successful, Gideon knew the Germans would be scouring the surrounding desert by air and on the ground once daylight came. The only possible way the Phoenix team could escape was by air.

Unfortunately, the sand surrounding the bunker was too soft for landing an airplane, and Said told Gideon the nearest possible landing site was two hours to the north by camel. Gideon requested that a plane be waiting for them at six a.m., just before sunrise. The plane was to wait ten minutes, then take off. If Phoenix was seriously delayed, they'd lose their only chance to escape the easy way.

In case they did have to try to cross the desert to Egypt, Gideon ordered extra food and water, along with a second Bedouin tent. These supplies would remain with the camels, which Masucci would guard.

By the time Gideon had finished encoding the message, Said had returned from hobbling the camels. Gideon verified the map coordinates of the drop zone and the rescue-plane rendezvous with the Bedouin. The Phoenix leader unwrapped the metal case that held the radio, opened it, and began transmitting. He'd send the message once tonight, then repeat it tomorrow night. To stay on the air longer would risk the Germans getting a fix on their location.

The next day, Gideon spotted a plane that seemed to have picked up the camel tracks, for it crisscrossed the sky to the west for over an hour. He expected to hear the sound of machine-gun fire at any moment when the pilot found the camels. But then the buzz of the plane's engines disappeared.

On the second day, they heard other planes, and Said, reconnoitering to the south, passed within a mile of a foot patrol. But by the third day, whatever enemy search had been launched seemed to be over.

Time became their enemy, passing like sand in the hourglass of the desert. The nights, though bitterly cold, were tolerable. Although they couldn't risk a fire, the men sat up and talked for hours about past battles and the mission to come. In'Hout and Gideon often played cards by moonlight, and to keep fit, they walked and did exercises.

The days, however, were unbearable. All they could do was lie under the burlap sacks beneath the torrid sun and try to sleep. But the heat was so stifling that sleep seldom came, and each man retreated into his own inner world.

For the first time since the creation of Phoenix, Gideon permitted himself to think about life after the war. His thoughts centered on Eliska Dobrensky, the Slovak woman who had joined the Phoenix team on a mission to recover a wealth of art from the Germans in Hungary.

Gideon's relationship with her had evolved slowly. At first it had been completely professional, as they fought side by side in a daring hundred-mile escape through divisions of enemy troops. Then had come passionate lovemaking, a confirmation of life among all the death they saw. Finally, they had arrived at a deep emotional commitment.

Gideon had feared his relationship with Eliska would make leading the Phoenix team in combat more difficult. Now, he thought, it made his job easier, since he was more determined than ever to bring his team through desperate missions unharmed. Emotion had not yet clouded his judgment.

Perhaps, he thought as he endured the misery of the desert, the risk they shared in combat was what really held him and Eliska together. After the war, when the danger had passed, would there be enough left between them to sustain their relationship, to build a civilian life together? For now, all he could look forward to was a night or two together before they plunged into the hell of the Nazi bunker.

After what seemed like an eternity, the sixth night came. Gideon, In'Hout, and Fuad El-Said moved to the drop zone and lit a flare at exactly two a.m. They stared upward at the star-studded sky, straining to hear the engines of an approaching aircraft.

They heard nothing that night. Nor the next two nights.

The tension on the ninth day was unbearable. Gideon knew that if they were to reach the bunker by three o'clock the next morning, the rest of Phoenix had to arrive now. If they didn't, the opportunity to strike at the Nazi menace would be lost.

During the endless, scorching day, Gideon mentally listed dozens of things that could have gone wrong—the radio message not getting through, the mission sabotaged by spies, and the plane being shot down. Hell, Gideon thought, for all he knew, Rommel could have invaded Egypt and captured Cairo.

In'Hout and the Italian were also caught in the agony of the wait. Only Said remained calm.

Finally, the sun descended toward the horizon. But as it dipped below the desert sands, the wind picked up. The sunset was dust-shrouded, and visibility dropped dramatically. Gideon feared that the plane, if it arrived, would be unable to see the flare. If the wind got even worse, the pilot might turn the craft back, fearing the parachutists might be blown miles from the drop site.

Blackness came. Gideon watched Said kneel for his evening prayers. The Bedouin's calmness only made Gideon realize how tense and nervous he felt, each minute stretching out agonizingly. The waiting was always the worst part of every mission.

They moved out to the drop site after midnight. In their bulky Bedouin robes, they sat in silence as the wind and sand whipped around them.

By one-forty a.m., the tension was extremely thick. In'Hout got to his feet and paced back and forth. Ten minutes later, Gideon joined him. They remained silent, concentrating on the small sounds carried by the gusty wind.

In'Hout suddenly stopped. "What's that?" he asked. "Do you hear it?"

Gideon listened intently.

"It's a motor. But I can't tell if it's on the ground or in the air."

Gideon strained to hear the noise, then spoke. "Airplane. Light the flares."

The wind had picked up again as Gideon crouched. The first three matches instantly blew out.

Said and Masucci joined them, forming a windbreak. Finally a flare caught, sizzling in the blackness.

Gideon used the burning flare to light the others. The four men hurried to place them in a square pattern, marking the jump zone.

The drone of the engine got louder. They stared upward into the dust-laden sky, hoping the flares could be seen.

Then, to their intense disappointment, the sound began to fade, and the flares to burn out.

"Did they miss us?" In'Hout asked.

"It could have been a German plane, for all we know," Gideon replied.

"What do we do?"

"I don't know. Maybe—"

"Again. It comes again!" Masucci exclaimed.

Gideon looked up. "There!" He pointed.

He'd seen a flash of white—it had to be a chute.

Said saw it, too. "West," he said. "We must get to them quickly."

They took off at a run. A few minutes later, they crested a large dune. In front of them was a parachute flapping like a luffing sail. At the other end of it a giant of a man was pulling on the cords.

"Brusilov!" Gideon yelled.

The towering Russian gave him a huge smile, which quickly faded to concern. "The others," he said out of breath. "The wind's taking them."

Gideon ran to help Brusilov out of his harness. In addition to the full rucksack on his back, the Russian carried a Bren machine gun and drums of the .303 ammo.

"Are we glad to see you!" Gideon told him. He shouted instructions over the wind to the rest. "Fan out! Follow the wind! Look for the other chutes!"

They ran downwind. Said spotted the next chute and was the first to reach it. The others caught up in a moment. It was Marcel Charvey, doubled up on the ground, his face cut and bruised.

The Frenchman looked up, saw Said first and started for his gun, then recognized Gideon's face.

"*Ah, c'est vous*, Gideon." Seeing In'Hout he added, "*Salut, Joel. Comment ça va?*"

Gideon and In'Hout, wearing broad smiles, bent over to help Charvey unstrap, while the others held down the flapping chute.

"You okay?" Gideon asked.

"Just got the wind knocked out of me. I was dragged."

"Can you walk?"

"I think so." Charvey staggered to his feet under the weight of the heavy pack.

"I'll carry that," Brusilov offered.

"No, I'll manage. You all go ahead and look for the others. I saw one chute above me. It should land somewhere over there." Charvey pointed.

The men ran northwest, spreading out and sweeping the area.

"There!" Masucci pointed toward the sky.

Gideon saw the white chute descending at an angle. He started running, trying to cut it off. In'Hout, to the north, was angling the other way in an attempt to intercept the dropping chute.

Gideon now saw the figure below the white. It was Kinelly. He hit the ground hard—gave at the knees and waist to absorb the impact, but lost his balance and footing. The billowing chute dragged him along the ground.

In'Hout leaped but just missed Kinelly's feet. Gideon, coming from the other direction, went for the chute, barreling into it and knocking the wind out. He went down in a tangle of cloth and cord.

Hands helped him up. It was Brusilov. In'Hout was at Kinelly's side, unstrapping him. The Irishman was unconscious but had a strong pulse.

"Stay with him," Gideon told In'Hout. He turned to the others who had gathered. "Eliska's out there somewhere. Spread out. But keep in shouting distance. We can't become separated."

The group moved out into the darkness. Fifteen minutes passed, occasional shouts the only sounds breaking through the roaring wind.

Suddenly Said's deep voice boomed, "A parachute! Just to the west!"

Gideon broke into a slow run, awkward against the fierce wind. The others followed.

Gideon reached the grounded chute first. A supply chute. He felt his heart plummet. "Cut the container loose," he ordered.

El-Said whipped out a curved knife and slashed the ropes.

Gideon stood and stared fixedly into the desert night. An image of Eliska being dragged along the desert floor rose in his mind like a nightmare. He tried, unsuccessfully, to suppress it. The grouping of the other chutes had been tight. What had happened?

"The storm's getting worse. In'Hout will have to take Kinelly back to the campsite and stay with him." Gideon motioned to Said. "Tell In'Hout. Show him the way back. The rest of us will keep searching for a while longer. We'll stay close together. Our only choice is to follow the wind. If we locate supplies on the way, we'll cut them free, mark the spot, and collect the containers on the way back. Any questions?"

The others nodded. There was nothing to say.

The wind died with the morning light. Reluctantly, Gideon ordered a return to the campsite. They had to get rest and water before resuming the search for Eliska, a search that seemed increasingly hopeless.

They had, however, found all but one of the supply containers. Each man carried a container as they trudged back to where In'Hout was tending Kinelly.

The Irishman was awake when they returned. He'd suffered a slight concussion, but the hours of sleep had left him with nothing more than a slight headache. He was ready for the mission.

Gideon waited until the men had replenished their bodies. Then he announced, "The attack is tonight. The supplies have to be uncrated and organized. Brusilov, you and Kinelly take care of that."

The Russian looked at him. "What about Eliska?"

Gideon's expression was grim. "The rest of us will go back out, despite the sun. In'Hout, get water, compasses, and burlap bags for everyone."

"Why the burlap bags?" Charvey asked.

"To hide under if a plane flies overhead."

Said added, "The search can last no longer than midday, five hours from now. For men unused to the desert, any longer would pose grave risk of heat exhaustion."

Gideon grimaced. "Okay. As badly as we want to find Eliska, the mission comes first. We'll need rest and time for a thorough briefing. Any questions?"

"I have one more suggestion," Said offered. "Last night

we searched to the northwest. But the wind can swirl west or even southward off the dunes. We should concentrate on that direction now."

"Good," Gideon said. He got to his feet. "Let's go."

Three hours later, Gideon trudged up another giant dune carved by the desert wind. The sun, climbing higher and higher in the sky, beat down on him unmercifully. His skin was raw despite the Bedouin robes, and his throat was dry and parched. His eyes ached from the glare.

An hour earlier, he'd spotted a parachute and had broken into a run. To his intense disappointment, it was the missing supply container. He'd kicked it in frustration. Then it came to him that the container was at least proof that the wind had shifted west at times. It gave him renewed incentive to push on through the stubborn sands.

He stopped for a mouthful of water from his rapidly dwindling supply, and swished it around his mouth, savoring it before swallowing.

Then he heard the chatter of automatic-weapon fire. He was so stunned that he spit the water out and dashed up to the top of the dune, machine pistol at the ready.

He saw nothing.

He waited five minutes. He was about to move on when he heard another burst, this time five or six shots that came from his left.

He broke into a run, ignoring his fatigue as his mind raced. One of the others must have run into a German patrol. But then why wasn't the air filled with the sounds of a fire fight?

He crossed a stretch of sandless rock, then ran up a tall dune. His legs ached from the exertion of climbing in the soft sand, and he grunted as he forced air into his lungs. At the top, he stumbled and rolled a third of the way down the other side.

He caught his breath before getting to his feet. In front of him, he saw hands brandishing a machine pistol.

A jolt went through him. Then the weapon dropped to the sand and a voice said, "Scott. Thank God."

Gideon ran down the dune and held her to him. "Are you all right?"

She nodded. "I landed without a problem. Except I had no idea where I was. I wandered around last night, but I decided my chances were better if I stayed put."

"Why did you fire your weapon? I could have been a German."

"Even a German would have been better than dying of hunger and thirst. I was beginning to get desperate."

"We were beginning to give up hope. We have so little time left. We have to destroy the German bunker tonight."

Eliska pulled away from him. "I have a caution for you from Philaix."

"What."

"He is well acquainted with this Ulmer, the director of the research project. Philaix engaged Ulmer's services as a consultant before the war. He says the German is an extraordinarily brilliant scientist who is the single unreplaceable element in Germany's rocket program."

"I knew that," Gideon said. "So what?"

"Philaix said to tell you it is vitally important to make sure Ulmer is killed when the bunker is blown up. He wants you to verify the death, as well as make absolutely sure the plans for the rocket are destroyed."

Gideon was silent for a few moments. "That's going to add to the time we're in the bunker. The mission is dangerous enough as it is."

"Philaix realizes that," Eliska said. Then she added with a smile, "He seems to think we have nine lives, like a cat."

"We're going to need them," Gideon said. "All of them."

CHAPTER NINE

THEY LAY AGAINST the slipface of a dune. Gideon pointed southeastward over the crest.

"That's the top of the escarpment, the roof of the bunker's upper level," he explained. "The air shaft leading down to the mess hall is about fifty or sixty yards from the escarpment's edge. Fortunately, we have cloud cover tonight."

"Any floodlights?" Brusilov asked.

"The Germans rely primarily on secrecy to protect the *Betonunterstand*," Gideon replied. "There are periscopes near the edge of the escarpment, and sporadic foot patrols. We'll approach the ledge from the south, then drop to the sand and crawl to the air shaft. We've got to be extremely careful—if we're spotted, a lift will hoist a battery of guns and floodlights to the surface."

"Bloody Christ," Kinelly swore. "How in the hell are we going to get out if they have a battery of guns on top?"

"That's Brusilov's job. While the rest of us descend, he'll wire the gun doors. If they're brought to the surface, they'll be blown up." Gideon turned to the Russian. "Brusilov, you'll set up the Bren at the top of the ledge. From there, you'll be able to pick off any SS troops coming out the doors in the rock face below. That's absolutely critical, because we're going to make our escape through the launch doors, a couple hundred meters out on the plain from the base of the escarpment."

"No problem," the Russian said.

Charvey spoke up. "Should we try to block the periscopes before we descend?"

"No," Gideon answered. "That would be a dead giveaway. The longer we remain undetected, the closer we get to the heart of the bunker, our target. If we're really lucky, the Germans won't know we've paid a visit until their whole goddam complex explodes."

"How are we getting down the air shaft?" Eliska asked.

"By rope," Gideon said, tapping the coil of wire-cored rope with a grappling hook at the end. "We'll have to cut the wire mesh at the top, then be careful not to bang against the stone walls while we descend. If our Hungarian friend Tibor Horvath has done his job, the fan will have been disabled and the grate removed so we can climb into the mess hall."

"What about after we get inside?" Said asked.

Gideon motioned with his hand. "Let's go down behind this dune face so I can review the layout of the bunker one more time."

The others followed Gideon. They huddled around him as he crouched down on one knee and drew a diagram in the sand with his knife. Then, pointing to each section as he spoke, Gideon dissected the bunker. This was the third time through for new arrivals. The others had been hearing about the bunker for days.

"Once again, the sliding doors in the face of the escarpment open into a huge storage room big enough for vehicles to drive into. The two towers are located on opposite side walls—the gun tower with the gun lift for surface action and the guard tower with machine-gun nests trained inside the room and on the front doors. At the very top there are periscopes for surface lookout. Behind the gun tower is a trapdoor leading to the emergency shaft to the lower level—inside there's a winch and a steel ladder fixed to the wall. On the back wall of the antechamber are the sliding doors to the upper passageway and upper rooms—the kitchen here, the mess hall, the various barracks and washrooms."

Gideon paused, picturing the bunker's interior in his mind, then continued. "An elevator at the end of the upper passageway leads to another directly below it. The lower one is much longer. It passes all the way back under the antechamber, out under the lower plain, and all the way to the launch vault. The doors along both sides"—Gideon ticked off boxes in his sand diagram one by one—"open up into the generator room, the well room, various laboratories, and right here, the lower end of the emergency shaft. Opposite the emergency shaft door is the entrance to a series of interconnecting machine shops. These rooms open up into an even larger chamber, the rocket-assembly room, which connects the main lower passageway to a second lower parallel passageway also leading to the launch vault. After the rockets are assembled, they're rolled through this alternate passageway to the launch pad. There's a single door off this passageway. It leads to the fuel-storage vault—you've all memorized the combination that the Germans passed on to Wolfgang Lichter?"

Eliska recited it.

"Good. Inside the vault are five separate compartments where various chemicals are stored. As for the launch vault, there's a circular pad with a walkway surrounding it. Between the two sets of doors leading to the parallel passageways is the control room equipped with periscopes to watch the launch. The controls to the launch doors are inside as well. A huge crane reaches to the top of the vault and is used by the Germans to bring in equipment too bulky and heavy to be brought in through the antechamber." Gideon thought a moment, making sure he had not overlooked anything. "That covers everything. Are there any questions?"

There were none.

"The place is a goddam labyrinth inside," Gideon warned. "You've got to know your way around, in case we run into trouble. We've got only forty-five minutes from the time we enter the air shaft until the explosives go off—any longer and the Germans will have us for sure."

"We'll set the timers before we descend?" In'Hout asked.

"No, we'll wait until we reach the fuel-storage tank. But we'll keep to our time schedule unless it's impossible for everyone to reach our target. If any one of you gets through, you're to set the explosives on schedule, even if the others have been delayed or have been taken prisoner."

Gideon paused while the others nodded grimly, fully aware of the dangers. "I'm reminding you of this especially because I won't be with you. I've got to make sure Semmeln Ulmer is dead—the threat of the XX rocket won't be totally eliminated unless we kill the man who created it, as well as blowing up the research facility. If I'm delayed, don't wait for me. That's an order."

There was silence for a moment. Then Charvey spoke out. "Let's run through exactly what we're likely to encounter once we reach the mess hall. Will it be guarded?"

"Horvath should be alone," Gideon answered. "But there will be four pairs of hallway guards. Our best bet is to lure them inside the mess hall and dispatch them. Then Horvath will go to the elevator, the only practical way down—you'd never make it through the antechamber to the emergency shaft. When you get to the bottom, you'll find twelve guards in the lower passageway. All we can count on to overtake them is surprise. Once you've dealt with the guards, destroy the elevator so the Germans can't use it."

"Where will you be?" Eliska asked.

"I'm going to see if Ulmer is in his room first. That's on the same level as the mess hall. If I find out he's below, I'll use the emergency shaft. I'll be in a German uniform, so I shouldn't have a problem. But remember again, don't wait for me or anyone else once you reach the five fuel-storage tanks. Just set the explosives."

The Phoenix members nodded.

Gideon continued. "Kinelly, Charvey, In'Hout, Said, you'll have the packs with the limpet mines. Eliska, you'll be carrying the spare ammo and grenades. If one of the others is wounded, you'll have to drop your pack and take the one with the mines."

"I understand," Eliska said.

"In'Hout, you've had the most time to familiarize yourself with the plans. You're in charge. You can take the others to the fuel-storage vault either through the machine shops and assembly room, or around through the launch vault. When you get there, the magnets on the limpets should make your job a quick one."

"Do we stagger our fuse settings to synchronize the moment of detonation as we go from tank to tank?" In'Hout asked.

"Yes," Gideon replied. "Say, two-minute intervals to go from tank to tank. And after you set the limpets, head to the launch vault. Horvath will hop in the cab of the crane and position it right below the launch doors at the surface. We'll start climbing the boom of the crane while Horvath goes to the control room and opens the doors above. He'll follow."

Gideon turned to Masucci. He had decided that the Italian youth would be the one to stay behind with the camels and the supplies. He had considered leaving Said behind as well, but he'd seen the Bedouin fight at close quarters and decided he would be more valuable in the bunker.

"Masucci," Gideon said, "I'll leave you my Sten, since I have an MP40. Stay alert. The most important part of your job is to protect that radio. If something goes wrong, it's the only chance we have to call for a pickup."

The young man nodded soberly. "I won't let you down."

Gideon turned back to the others. He could sense they were ready for action.

"Let's go."

This is when we need the goddam wind, Gideon thought bitterly as they crawled on their bellies along the rugged edge of the escarpment. With just a little wind stirring up the dust, their dark shapes would have been obscured even more. At least they had the cloud cover, blocking out the moon and stars.

The going was slow and painful with the heavy loads on their backs. Only Said wore the layers of Bedouin clothing; everyone else was dressed in dark sweaters and slacks for mobility and nighttime camouflage. Underneath his clothing Gideon wore the Waffen SS uniform—he didn't want to risk soiling it, which might give him away. Once inside the bunker, he'd remove his outer garments.

By Gideon's estimation, they were about two-hundred yards from the gun doors. They would separate from Brusilov in another fifty yards and angle off toward the ventilation shaft.

Suddenly, the ground dropped out from under Gideon and the upper part of his body pitched forward. He gasped, stifling a cry for help, as he stared down into blackness. Brusilov quickly grabbed Gideon's feet, pulling him back to safety before he tumbled over the edge and down the face of the escarpment.

Collecting himself, Gideon shook his head at the close call. The ledge wasn't perfectly straight, but angled inward in places. He had nearly crawled into a crevice.

He took a deep breath, then started moving again, a little farther inward from the edge. He was pulling with his elbows, which cradled his weapon, and pushing with his knees and feet. The others followed, squirming through the soft sand that bordered the rocky edge of the precipice.

Gideon stopped to change course toward the air shaft, sending Brusilov on alone. Then he heard a noise, a scuffling sound off to the left. He froze, as did the others.

The sound of jackboots in the sand meant they were not alone on the escarpment. A night patrol was coming directly toward them.

He strained to pick out the shapes. Against the slightly lighter sky he could see six men moving in single file near the gun doors ahead.

He glanced at his watch: two forty-four. In sixteen minutes they should be at the air shaft. Horvath would be making his move for the vent. And if Phoenix was delayed, every additional moment would increase the odds of his being discovered.

Gideon watched the guards, willing them away. They angled southeastward over the bunker's roof and toward the edge of the escarpment where they stopped and looked out at the plain below.

Gideon held his breath. The Nazis were heading west, right toward Phoenix.

He checked his watch. Nine minutes to go.

"Knives ready. Leave packs. Pass it on," Gideon whispered. He reflected for a moment. Six guards. Seven of them.

"Everyone take a man," he ordered. "Said, you back us up with your sword. Here they come."

The Phoenix team crouched, ready to spring. The Germans would be passing to their left, away from the ledge.

By keeping an eye on one another, they were able to jump their men at nearly the same time. The move they had practiced so often at Bladesover came naturally—grab the mouth from behind with the left hand and thrust the knife in the jugular with the right. But the timing had to be perfect. If the thrust was made too late, a strong or agile man could break the hold by jerking his body down and flipping the attacker.

It happened to Eliska. Her hold was too low and her thrust missed. The German pulled his chin away, grabbed her left arm, and yanked her over his shoulder. Rather than resist and have her arm broken, Eliska went with the motion, landing on her back in the soft sand.

The German didn't raise the alarm. Instead, he bent down for his machine pistol, raised himself back up, and focused his weapon on Eliska. Before he could fire, Said swung his Tuareg sword and sliced off the man's head.

Gideon's target had spun out of his grasp, knocking the Phoenix leader off balance. Steadying himself, Gideon kicked the man's feet out from under him and flung himself at the fallen German. The Nazi tried to crawl away, but Gideon smashed the back of his neck. He put both hands behind the soldier's head and pressed it down into the sand. The man struggled violently for air, but Gideon, with both knees planted firmly, had the leverage to bear down with all of his weight. The man's struggles grew rapidly weaker. Then he went limp, suffocated in the sand.

The others had taken their men on the first attempt. Moving low to the ground, they returned to their packs. Gideon, Eliska, and Said hurried to join them.

Crouching, they strapped the rucksacks to their backs.

Gideon checked the time. Four and a half minutes. Time was running out.

"Brusilov, we separate here. You keep crawling along the ledge toward the gun doors. The rest of us will walk upright. If the Germans spot us, they'll think we're the patrol. Hurry."

Brusilov, cradling the Bren, moved out on his stomach. Gideon led the others on a sweep—first north, then east, so they'd be facing the periscopes head-on as they approached the ventilation shaft. With the packs, their profiles would give them away.

They reached the air shaft one minute late. Horvath should have done his work by now.

But the fan was still on, its motor humming, its blades drawing air. A host of questions bombarded Gideon's brain. Was this the right air shaft? Had his signals with Horvath gotten crossed? Had Horvath been discovered? Should they descend the shaft and try to blow up the fan? Try to breach the bunker elsewhere? Any variation in the plan would be suicidal.

Then the fan stopped, the motor cutting out. Horvath had come through.

"Quickly, Charvey. Cut the mesh," Gideon ordered.

The Frenchman set to work on the wire screening enclosing the vent below the domed, sand-dappled cover. The sound of the wire cutters snipping through the metal seemed to resound through the desert silence.

Gideon readied the grapple. When Charvey had cut a hole big enough for a man with a rucksack, Gideon wrapped the rope twice around the vent, then secured two of the grapple's claws in the remaining mesh.

"Synchronize watches," Gideon whispered. "Fifteen seconds to three-oh-five. The explosives will be set for exactly three-fifty."

The others set their watches.

"In'Hout," Gideon ordered, "you first. Give two tugs when you reach bottom."

The acrobatic Dutchman grabbed the line and maneuvered through the hole. He began to lower himself hand over hand, his feet braced against the shaft's inner wall. It was bumpy and jagged; the Germans evidently saw no reason to smooth the shaft with metal tubing or concrete. The rucksack caught on the rough surface, making the descent even more difficult. In'Hout's arms began to ache.

The shaft was pitch-black. After what seemed like an eternity, In'Hout felt a flat surface.

A light clicked on briefly, illuminating his surroundings. "Hurry!" a voice mumured.

In'Hout tugged the rope twice. In the flash of light he had seen a space between two blades of a huge fan. He ducked through it, sidled past the grate that had been unscrewed and propped a few feet to one side, and stepped out onto the floor of the mess hall. Tibor Horvath, standing close by in the darkness, greeted him with a whisper.

"Welcome to the *Betonunterstand*."

Gideon felt the two yanks on the rope and sent Charvey down. Kinelly would follow. Gideon wanted to get all the explosives down first. He would descend after Kinelly—he needed time to confer with Horvath—and Eliska and Said would go last.

Gideon looked for Brusilov along the escarpment's edge, but couldn't make him out. Good. The Germans on the periscopes also would have a hard time seeing the big Russian.

Gideon's turn came. He grabbed the rope, maneuvered feet first through the hole, and lowered himself into the darkness.

A light shining through the grate illuminated Gideon's last ten feet. He hit bottom, tugged the rope twice, and found the space between the fan blades. Charvey helped him as he stepped out onto the concrete floor. The light clicked off again. Another hand reached out of the dark to grasp his.

"You made it," Horvath whispered.

"Yes, good work. Two more team members to get down and we're on our way. Listen, I want you to lead the others to the fuel-storage vault. Are there eight guards in the hall as usual?"

"Right."

"How did you get by them?"

"I created a diversion. I started a fire in one of the barracks earlier. In the smoke and confusion, I slipped away. I have been hiding here for hours."

"Where's your personal guard?"

"Dead. In the generator room." Horvath's tone was solemn but there was an underlying note of exhilaration.

"Do you think you can draw the guards in here?" Gideon asked.

"Not all of them. Some of them will stay outside to keep an eye on the hall."

"See what you can do. After we deal with them, I want you to call the elevator, then kill the operator."

"Bad idea. At this time of night, the door is probably already open on this level. The operator will see the guards come in here and then me coming out alone. He'll get suspicious."

Gideon hadn't thought of that. He began removing his outer clothing, then grabbed the SS helmet out of his pack. "I'll handle him. You be ready to follow with the others. Then I'm going for Ulmer. I'll join up with you later. Do you know where he is?"

"Probably in his room at this hour, but maybe not. It is said he's an insomniac."

Gideon's tone was deadly earnest. "I'll find him."

Eliska had reached the bottom and emerged from the vent; Said was working his way down. Gideon, quickly shining his light ahead long enough to get a fix on the door, the aisle, the table and benches, hurried across the mess hall. The others—all except Eliska, who stayed behind to help Said out of the air shaft—followed.

"Call the guards in," Gideon instructed Horvath. "Tell them it's an emergency. You were inspecting the electrical system for fire damage—that's why the power is out—and you found an air shaft with its grate removed. Not too loud or you might wake others. Walk toward them if you have to."

The Hungarian opened the door and looked up and down the long, tubular passageway. Incandescent bulbs cast a yellow swath of light through the door onto the porous floor. The Phoenix team sank even farther back into the shadows.

"Be ready with your knives," Gideon whispered.

"*D'accord*," Charvey muttered.

They heard Horvath speaking in German down the hall. Then footsteps—jackboots clicking on concrete.

Two Germans entered. The Phoenix members engulfed them, going for their faces to suppress any shouts for help and jamming knives into their torsos. The Germans crumpled to the mess-hall floor.

Horvath was back at the open door with a hasty warning.

"Four more are coming down the hall. Thirty seconds." He closed the door as In'Hout and Charvey dragged the bodies away from it.

"We'll use our guns as clubs this time," Gideon suggested. "The moment all four are through the door. Just before we strike, Eliska will shine a light in their faces to blind them. Said, you help where needed.

Gideon, In'Hout, Kinelly, and Charvey stood in pairs opposite each other, a gauntlet of four, guns ready. Eliska and Said stood at the end, but far enough away from the door to be out of the wedge of light, when it opened. They listened for the sound of approaching jackboots.

"In here, hurry," Horvath directed them from behind the door. "I'll turn on my light."

The four guards rushed in. Phoenix guns slashed down, hitting faces and necks. Men grunted in pain. One cried out. Machine pistols clattered to the floor. Phoenix struck again, then jumped back. Said joined the battle, brandishing his sword. He made four quick slices, hitting each guard once.

Only one remained standing, staggering toward Eliska. His neck and shoulder were bloody. He yelled. Eliska smashed him across the face with the flashlight, then kicked up into his groin. Hands to his face, he doubled up. Kinelly finished him off with a tremendous blow to the back of his head, just below his helmet.

Horvath was looking down the hall through the open door.

"Did the others hear?" Gideon asked.

"Yes, they're coming with their guns ready."

"Quick, Horvath, stand in the light. I'll stand to one side pointing my gun at you as if you're my prisoner. That'll confuse them for a moment, long enough for the rest of you to close in. Let's not blow it now. Don't let them get a shot off."

They took up positions and waited. The last two guards didn't rush into the mess hall the way the others had, but stopped at the door and peered cautiously around the frame. They saw Horvath standing with his hands up.

"What is this?" one of them asked in German.

"A traitor to the Fatherland," Gideon replied, spitting the German words out to disguise his voice.

"*Ja?*" The two soldiers entered the room.

Phoenix pounced. Charvey got his gun around one man's neck and pulled back hard, snapping his spinal cord. In'Hout and Kinelly dispatched the other guard, hitting him high and low with gun and knife.

Eight dead. So far so good. Still no alarm. Now for the elevator. Gideon wondered for a moment whether the rest of the team should take the uniforms from the dead, but decided against it—it would take too much time and the rucksacks would give them away anyway. Gideon did, however, grab up a haversack with stick grenades for himself.

"Be ready to follow. Cover me if necessary," he said, then rushed out the door and broke into a trot.

The guard in the elevator had obviously been following the activity in the hall with interest. He stood at the doors, gazing in Gideon's direction, confused to see a guard running in his direction. His craggy face was flushed and he had his finger on the trigger of his MP40.

Gideon gauged the closing distance. Thirty more strides until he'd be in striking range . . . twenty . . .

"We have to go down," he called out in German to distract the man.

Ten strides . . .

"*Warum? Ich*—" the German started to say, but before he could finish Gideon plowed into him, knocking him down.

The man was quick and squirmed out from under Gideon. He started to shout, but Gideon, lashing out, jammed the barrel of his MP40 into the man's mouth. The German, his head driven backward, gagged. Gideon sprang onto him and hit him in the face repeatedly with the butt of his gun until the man no longer moved.

He turned to wave the others forward, but they were already running toward him. They reached the elevator and piled in. Horvath went for the controls. Gideon reached in the back of In'Hout's rucksack, took out two limpets, and stuffed them in his Waffen SS jacket.

"Okay, see you down below," he said, stepping back out into the passageway. "Get those explosives planted."

Six serious faces stared back at him as the doors slid shut. The motors whirred into life, and the elevator began its long descent, carrying a carload of death.

Gideon turned away, exhilarated. The explosives were on their way down, and he was on his way to find Ulmer. He looked at his watch. Three-eighteen a.m. It had been only thirteen minutes since In'Hout first went down the air shaft.

Christ, he thought, it seemed like an eternity.

CHAPTER TEN

THE HOIST MOTOR hummed to a stop. The elevator doors parted.

Four Waffen SS *Schützen*, in the usual gray-green combat uniforms and armed with the standard-issue MP40, stood facing the elevator. Phoenix opened fire, four automatics plus Said's Reveilli spewing forth hot, deadly lead. The guards toppled to the floor without getting off a single shot.

Down the hall, eight other guards, shocked out of their nighttime lethargy, spun their guns in reaction. At this distance, one man had an advantage—the Bedouin with his rifle. He was able to pick off the enemy guards as they tried to advance down the passageway.

A klaxon blared in the distance. Guards would be pouring forth from both the antechamber and the barracks above.

"Kinelly, Eliska, Charvey, quick, plant three limpets in the elevator with forty-one-second clocks," In'Hout ordered. He had timed the elevator ride.

Three soldiers were making progress in their advance by using the laboratory doorways as cover. Said maintained his sharpshooting from a kneeling position, forcing them to rush their shots. But they were now in automatic-fire range.

"Limpets ready to activate," Charvey announced.

"Get in the elevator," In'Hout told Said as he himself pulled the pins on two hand grenades. "Behind me. Horvath, prepare to send up the elevator. Everybody else get ready to activate the explosives and charge. We're going for the machine shop. One, two . . . go!"

In'Hout rushed out the elevator and, as if bowling, rolled first one and then the other grenade down the hall. Said ran behind him, blindly firing his rifle over the Dutchman. Kinelly, Eliska, and Charvey hit the buttons on the three limpets and charged after the other two men, automatics ready. Horvath hit the control button to send the elevator to the upper level.

The grenades detonated in resounding blasts, amplified in the confines of the passageway. Phoenix ran side by side behind a wall of lead, all except Horvath, who was a few steps behind.

They heard a distant, muffled explosion and thought of Brusilov on the upper level. Then a much louder sound assaulted their ears, the limpets detonating in the elevator. A moment later, there came a screaming noise—metal on metal—as the enclosed platform plummeted downward inside the shaft. It hit bottom with a wrenching crash.

The Phoenix members ran on, still another German falling before their guns. In'Hout counted. Four Germans dead at the elevator, two shot by Said, three killed by grenades, one before and another just now by automatic fire—out of the original twelve, that left one more of the guards for the lower-level passageway.

"How far to the machine shop?" he called back to Horvath.

"Far. Keep going."

They pumped their legs with every ounce of strength they could muster. The klaxon still was blaring, closer and louder now.

Then it stopped. The sudden silence seemed deafening. No klaxon, no explosions, no gunfire—only their footsteps, clomping on the concrete floor.

They passed door after door.

Finally, Horvath yelled, "Next one on the right!"

At that instant, the emergency-shaft door ahead opened and five soldiers—the first wave from the antechamber above—appeared.

Phoenix guns were ready for them, raking them before they

could level their weapons. The door slammed shut, then slowly opened again. The second wave of Germans was playing it more cautiously.

As the others dashed into the machine shop, Kinelly ran along the opposite wall, activated a grenade, and tossed it through the partially opened door of the shaft. He flattened against the wall as the explosion boomed inside, then hightailed it back after his friends.

In'Hout waited at the door of the machine shop, covering him. They both entered, slamming the heavy armored-steel door behind them. There was no lock on it, but the door opened on hinges into the room and could be barricaded shut. Horvath had turned on the overhead lights. In'Hout looked around him at the collection of heavy equipment. Nearby, on wheels, was a huge machine press. Perfect.

"Come on. Let's push this thing in front of the door!" In'Hout said, running toward it. "Horvath, Eliska, scout ahead through the assembly room. We'll be along."

Eliska and Horvath ran through the maze of machinery toward the opposite door leading to the rocket-assembly room, and beyond that, the second lower passageway, where they would find their ultimate target, the fuel-storage vault. On reaching the door leading out of the machine shop, Eliska stood ready with her Sten gun while Horvath opened it.

Darkness inside.

"Where are the lights?" she asked.

"On the inside wall," Horvath said, moving through the doorway toward the switch.

Shots rang out, a flurry of automatic fire. Horvath jumped back into the machine shop.

Eliska stuck the barrel of her Sten through the door and raked the room blind. She heard her bullets bouncing off metal parts. A machine pistol answered back.

"One gun, just one gun, aimed at the door," Eliska said. "We have to flush it out. You have no gun?"

Horvath shook his head. "I should have taken one off a dead guard."

"You're going to have to fight now," she said in Hungarian

to reassure him. Then she swung her gun around the frame and opened up again into the rocket-assembly room.

Once again, the single machine pistol volleyed back with an accurate burst. The bullets crashed off the open door a few feet from them.

In'Hout rushed up behind them, the rest of the team on his heels.

"How many?" the Dutchman asked.

"Just one, with a machine pistol trained at the door."

"The twelfth hallway guard. We can't waste any time. We have to get to the vault. We'll all go at once. One of us will get him. On the count of three. One, two—"

Just then the door on the opposite side of the assembly room opened, and lights clicked on in the huge room. German soldiers poured into the room and fanned out behind the piles of rocket parts. Rather than trying to break through the barricaded door, the third wave of guards from the emergency shaft had worked their way through the launch vault, along the far passageway, and into the assembly room, effectively blocking Phoenix's path to the fuel-storage vault. They'd never make it across the big room and through the far door. And the soldiers would keep coming down the emergency shaft and setting up more and more positions.

In'Hout, furious at himself for letting this happen, swore as he went for the door. He slammed it shut as enemy bullets ricocheted off it.

"We need another barricade," he said. "We're trapped."

Brusilov hefted the Bren machine gun as he wriggled stealthily over the sand toward the gun doors. The rest of the team would be inside the bunker by now. Every moment of continued silence meant they were penetrating deeper toward the volatile fuel.

He had to be getting closer. There would be a large rectangular depression in the sand with a rock rim. The surface of the doors would be granular—sand mixed with light-brown paint. If he kept on this straight course, running about twenty feet from the edge, he would be sure to come upon it. If he saw the periscope sticking out of the sand, he would know he had gone too far.

The night wasn't pitch-black—more like a dark gray with the drifting cloud cover—and Brusilov could still make out shapes as far as fifty feet away. Nonetheless, he listened intently for a patrol as he inched over the sand.

Just as his groping hands found the hard edge of a rock ridge protruding from the sand and, beyond and below it, what felt like grainy metal, he heard the sound of leather squeaking. At his fingertips, the gun doors. Maybe forty-five feet to the northeast, he figured, straining to look in the direction of the sound, another patrol. Six men. Too many for one man to eliminate silently.

Brusilov analyzed the situation while he slowly and silently angled the barrel of the Bren in the patrol's direction. There were four possible scenarios: He could be spotted and attacked, in which case he'd have to fight, most likely alerting the bunker; the corpses of the other patrol would be discovered, which would amount to the same thing; the patrol would stay up here, keeping watch, delaying his wiring of the gun doors; or it would go away.

The patrol angled off toward where Brusilov guessed the periscope was, stopped, then moved to the edge of the escarpment for a look at the plain below. Brusilov was beginning to understand the pattern of the Waffen SS patrols. They probably came out the front doors and walked in a straight line across the plain as far as the launch doors, then made a wide sweep either east or west to where the escarpment was climbable. Up top, they probably circled north, then back around south to the roof of the bunker from where they could check the plain again.

If Brusilov had figured correctly, all he had to do was wait a few minutes, and the patrol would depart.

He wormed his way back from the gun doors, in case the Germans decided to check them, retracing ground he had just covered. When he had reached what he considered to be a safe distance, he stopped to wait the Germans out.

For some reason, this patrol, unlike the other one, remained at the edge of the escarpment, gazing out over the desert floor below.

Five minutes passed. Brusilov agonized more and more with each passing second. Just two more minutes and he'd attack, rushing the Germans out of the shadows, knocking three over the ledge with the first thrust, finishing the others with his knife.

His dilemma made Brusilov appreciate what Gideon dealt with as their leader. The Russian could make split-second decisions, in the heat of battle. But this sort of protracted predicament was enough to . . .

The patrol was moving again, heading along the ledge toward the gun doors. The six soldiers examined the barriers, then continued westward in Brusilov's direction.

If they were going to spot him, it would be now. There would be a shout, then the blaze of guns.

But the patrol kept moving right past him. All heads seemed to be turned to the left, their eyes taking in the view below and not the dark profile on the desert floor just twenty meters to their right—a big man on his belly with a rucksack on his back.

The German patrol faded out of earshot. Time to act. Brusilov quickly slid out of his pack and placed the Bren gun on top of it to keep it from the sand. Then he removed four of his six limpets, plus fuses, and started crawling back to the gun doors. He felt ahead for the telltale rock rim.

There it was, and the sand-painted, steel-armored door panels just beyond and below it. Feeling for contours, he decided how to place the limpets. In addition to the clockwork fuses, Brusilov had brought along some time pencils from Cairo. With these, the moment of detonation was determined by the thickness of the fuse wire. When the fuses were broken, acid would eat through the wire, reaching the plastics at different times. Brusilov had shaved the pencil fuses down so that they would detonate one minute after being snapped. He would prop the limpets on the rock rim around the door, two to a side, with the fuses strung over the metal edges. When the doors were opened all the way, reaching their stops, the fuses would be activated. One minute later, when the platform of artillery had risen to the surface, the payoff—an explosion of fireworks.

Brusilov planted the first two limpets where he wanted them, with time pencils angled down, then turned around to crawl to the other end of the rectangle. Just as he crossed the seam where the two doors met, he heard the dreaded sound of an alarm—a screaming klaxon—in the antechamber below him. Seconds later, he heard a whirring, rumbling noise and felt the doors moving under him.

This was it.

Brusilov jumped up and ran away from the limpets he had already planted, his strides carrying him twice as fast as the door panel moved. He looked ahead for motionless ground, hurdled the rim onto it, and kept running. Behind him, against the shrill noise of the klaxon, he heard the sounds of the doors banging into the stops. The two limpets would be activated. The platform of guns would be rising. One minute now.

Brusilov suddenly veered leftward, circling back on a wide arc toward his pack and gun. He wouldn't make it in time, but at least he could get closer. For the moment, he carried only the two limpets he hadn't managed to plant and half a dozen grenades hooked onto his belt.

When he saw the first rays from the platform's floodlights rising above the desert surface, he dove for the sand.

The platform clanged into place, its battery of guns on the surface. A beacon's beam swept toward Brusilov.

He grabbed a grenade off his belt and flung it toward the bright light. It detonated short of the platform, kicking up only sand, doing no damage. A gun—it sounded to Brusilov like a Flakvierling 2cm quadruple—answered back, its bullets whizzing to the right of the Russian.

Then a violent blast dwarfed the noises of both the grenade and quadruple gun, coupled with a searing, golden, crescent-shaped flash of fire—the plastics—followed by leaping, darting tendrils of flame as the thermite incendiary ignited.

In quick succession, there came a distant, muffled explosion, like a faint echo. More of Phoenix's handiwork, Brusilov thought, deep in the bunker.

Men were screaming and shouting on the gun platform. Their numbers had been cut in half. Survivors battled the blaze with fire extinguishers. Brusilov could see amid the smoke and flames that the two limpets had blown out three of the four lights and knocked two of the four 88s off their mounts, as well as destroying some of the smaller-caliber guns. But once the fire was brought under control, there would be plenty of firepower left, certainly enough to blast the Phoenix team to pieces when they tried to escape through the launch doors on the desert plain below. He also spotted a pile of artillery shells neatly stacked between the two intact 88s. He had to get to that ammo before the Germans got to him.

Jumping up, Brusilov ran directly for the platform. As he moved, he stuck one of the two limpets on the back of the other and two grenades on the one still-exposed magnet. Bullets kicked up sand at his feet. He veered to the left, pulled the pins on the grenades, heaved the package at the pile of ammunition, and kept running.

The force of the explosion was like a giant fist walloping Brusilov from behind. He smashed to the ground face-first and tasted sand. Ears ringing, body aching, he turned around to see the two 88s that had survived the first explosion topple over the ledge, their huge shapes plummeting and spinning downward like prehistoric monsters herded over a cliff by fire. The giant behemoths banged against the rock face and crashed to the sand below, sending up spumes of dust.

Brusilov staggered up and broke into a limping run. The heat from the burning thermite and molten metal was so intense that he had to detour far around the inferno.

Finally, he reached his rucksack and gun and dragged them to the edge of the escarpment. He set the Bren on its bipod mount, slipped a 100-round drum into place, put the change lever on automatic, pulled back the cocking handle, and pushed it forward, folding it against the receiver. Below, soldiers were already streaming out and running toward the launch doors. Brusilov lined up the rest of his ammo, grenades, and last two limpets close by. The explosives would come in handy in case any Germans tried to scale the rock face to get to him. Then he lay flat behind the Bren, placed the butt against his right shoulder, grabbed the folding butt handle with his left hand and the pistol grip with his right, aimed, and squeezed the trigger.

It was like having his own personal shooting gallery.

The alarm went off just as Gideon, disguised in his Waffen SS uniform, reached Semmeln Ulmer's door. Down the hall, guards rushed out of the antechamber.

He tried the latch. As far as Gideon knew, all rooms in *Betonunterstand*—except the fuel-storage vault—were kept unlocked to enable the Waffen SS to make spot checks. This was no exception, even though it belonged to the director of the project. But the room was empty. If Ulmer had used his bed tonight, he had taken the time to remake it. In any case, he might now be anywhere in the bunker. Gideon had to ask someone. He hurried back into the hall.

Soldiers, armed to the teeth, rushed past him, heading for the elevator. No one paid attention to him. It made sense that a guard would look for Ulmer when an alarm went up. As long as no one recognized his face.

Gideon grabbed the arm of a soldier, stopping him in his tracks. It was a young man with a pimply, adolescent face, pinched tight with fervor and excitement. The *Betonunterstand* was probably his first hitch, and this his first action.

"*Wo ist Semmeln Ulmer? Wissen Sie?*" Gideon shouted, trying to be heard over the wailing siren.

"*Das Vorzimmer,*" the young soldier answered, then ran on down the hall, anxious to make the first elevator.

The antechamber! Good. Ulmer was close at hand.

Glancing left at the troops waiting for the elevator, Gideon turned the opposite way against the flow of traffic. Keep waiting and keep coming to this dead end, he thought smugly as he pushed through toward the antechamber door. There's no elevator coming.

But to his complete dismay, he heard a mass cheer from the other end of the passageway. He turned to look. Goddammit, he thought. The elevator had arrived at the upper level, and troops were piling in it for the ride down. Why had Phoenix let it come up?

Suddenly, a powerful blast erupted from the antechamber, followed by a second roaring crash and a blinding flash of light. It came right at Gideon, the shock wave like a huge shell knocking him down. Brusilov, Gideon thought with satisfaction.

It took Gideon a moment to clear his head and sort out what had happened. For a moment he had thought the whole bunker was going up prematurely. But now he understood. When the alarm had gone off, the gun platform had risen and set off Brusilov's charge—the first explosion. As for the second, the Phoenix members below had planted limpets on the elevator, blowing it up and eliminating some of the enemy in one stroke.

Gideon stood up shakily and looked both ways.

There were piles of lacerated bodies at the far end of the hall, some of them still burning from the thermite incendiary and sending forth a noxious odor. The passageway was a blackened shambles with twisted and jagged metal sticking out from what was once the elevator shaft. The elevator itself was gone, having plummeted below when the cables snapped.

Guards with fire extinguishers and scientists rushed past Gideon in all directions. One more ripping explosion then erupted from the antechamber. Gideon guessed it was Brusilov again, finishing off the gun battery.

Gideon reached the doorway at the end of the passageway and pushed past oncoming guards. They jostled him, but, in the confusion, no one looked too closely at his face.

The antechamber was filled with Germans. Gideon checked faces one by one in search of Ulmer. He saw that the SS captain who had first checked him into the *Betonunterstand* was trying to divide his troops into groups—two firefighting units for the elevator shaft and for the top of the gun tower, now a mess of mangled, smoking debris; and three attack units for the emergency shaft, the launch doors, and what remained of the elevator shaft. The men ran back and forth in front of the guard tower, joining their respective groups. When each unit had at least four men, it moved out on its particular assignment. Fresh soldiers, coming out of the guard tower or piling in from the crowded passageway, fell into line to await their instructions. On the various levels of the open steel guard tower, machine gunners sat in their nests, viewing the scene below.

The last of the firefighters moved out. Another group headed for the trapdoor behind the gun tower, leading to the emergency shaft. Still another headed for the front doors. The huge panels rumbled open, exposing the desert night. Just outside the doors, crumpled in the sand, two 88s that had crashed down from up above smoldered with thermite. The soldiers briefly stopped to examine them, then ran over the desert plain toward the launch doors.

A maching gun suddenly opened up outside—Brusilov's Bren on the ledge, aimed down at the running soldiers. The Germans pirouetted in a dance of death, none of them getting through. The Russian was carrying out his end of the plan. Now Gideon must act. He'd have to ask someone again about Ulmer.

A small armored personnel carrier, a half-track, was parked just inside the bunker's front doors. A group of soldiers, their arms laden with supplies, ran out the bottom level of the guard tower toward it. Colonel Steg was leading them.

Gideon spotted a civilian in the middle of this group—a man with gray hair, a wide face, and a high brow. Ulmer! The standing order from Berlin must be: If the XX rocket project falls under attack, evacuate the one man who can establish another. Gideon had arrived none too soon. In another minute Ulmer would have been gone.

Gideon broke into a run, heading for the half-track. Ulmer, Steg, and a driver climbed into the front. The rest piled in the back or grabbed handholds outside. The engine started up.

To get to the vehicle in time and grab hold, Gideon had to run past a captain who knew his identity. If he could just hop aboard, then all he had to do was stay with the half-track long enough to plant his limpets near Ulmer. Then he could jump off before detonation and sneak back into the bunker.

The personnel carrier was starting a slow turn out of the antechamber. Gideon rushed past the captain, and passed the front of the guard tower, where eight soldiers stood waiting for their attack orders. Thirty feet more, he estimated, and he'd reach the vehicle.

Suddenly, a German voice boomed out, *"Hei! Vorsicht!"* It was the SS captain.

One guard jumped forward, thrusting his legs under Gideon. The American crashed hard to the concrete floor. Other guards piled on top of him. Through the wall of jackboots, he saw the half-track accelerating through the bunker doors—Ulmer, escaping.

"Hierdurch!" the captain ordered, stepping into the office at the bottom of the guard tower.

The guards picked Gideon up and stood him on his feet. They stripped his MP40 from his arms and unstrung his haversack and grenades. Waving their guns, they pushed Gideon through the door. He pretended to lose his balance and fall forward over the doorsill and into the room. All eight guards followed him inside.

As he fell, Gideon reached into his Waffen SS jacket. When he stood, he held a limpet in one hand and the dial of a clockwork fuse attached to it in his other.

"Throw your guns down or this goes off," he threatened in German, setting the clock for one second. All he had to do was hit the button.

The soldiers looked to their captain, who stood next to a desk. He nodded, his once sneering face now panic-stricken. All eight men dropped their weapons.

Gideon edged past the soldiers toward the door.

"The men outside will shoot you," the captain told him. "There are too many for you."

"Who will give the order?" Gideon asked, and in one sudden, smooth motion, he dropped the limpet and stepped through the door.

He flattened himself against the outside wall a pulsebeat before the explosion ravaged the room and the men inside. The force of the blast through the corrugated-metal wall knocked him forward.

Staggering up, he spotted a fire extinguisher propped against the corner pylon of the guard tower. He sprinted for it, grabbed it, then pivoted back toward the door. He began spraying the thermite blaze inside. The explosion had drawn the attention of other guards in the antechamber. Those waiting their turn to descend the emergency shaft turned to watch. Others on the upper levels of the guard tower leaned over their railings to check the action immediately below. Gideon hoped that no one would suspect a man of starting a fire if he was trying to put it out.

"It's no use," he yelled in German to the guards above him. "I can't contain it. You'd better evacuate your posts."

The billowing, noxious smoke rising from the office convinced them. They ran to the far corner of the tower, away from the office, to descend the latticed pylon.

Gideon looked around, planning his next move. There was no getting to Ulmer now. He had failed in that endeavor. When Phoenix got out of here, they could pick up his trail. Now it was time to concentrate on the destruction of the bunker.

Gideon set off in a run toward the emergency shaft. On the way, he saw the remainder of a group of soldiers disappearing through the trapdoor. Evidently there were no Phoenix members on the other end.

Gideon made a quick decision. He'd take the emergency shaft and the soldiers in it, then use the elevator shaft to descend. Still on the run, he pulled out his last limpet and set the fuse for seven seconds—the time, he judged, it would take for him to exit the antechamber.

On reaching the trapdoor, he looked around one more time. He ducked his head as a group of scientists entered the big vaulted antechamber from the hall. Any of them might recognize him. They ran past him toward the front doors. He hoped Brusilov would pick them off if they tried to escape.

His Bren was still chattering outside. Gideon wondered with sudden hope if Brusilov had possibly managed to stop the half-track carrying Ulmer. The Bren had been firing pretty steadily.

It was time to move, with confusion still reigning.

Gideon lifted the trapdoor. Then, using his body to shield his hands, he activated the limpet and dropped it down the shaft. He slammed the door back down and ran for the passageway.

Still another explosion rocked the *Betonunterstand*. Gideon, moving down the hallway at full speed, imagined bodies being blow into tiny pieces, the steel ladder buckling and cracking, thermite igniting human flesh, smoke rising.

There were guards at the end of the passageway, entering the wreckage of the elevator shaft one by one. Gideon bent over a dead soldier to pick up an MP40 and several spare magazines. Then he ran on ahead and fell in line. The astringent smoke and fumes stung his eyes and lungs. Coughing, he wiped his face.

He checked behind him. There were no other soldiers in the passageway at the moment, but there would be soon as this was the only remaining route down. It wouldn't be long before a new commanding officer brought the chaos in the antechamber under control.

Gideon waited until all but one of the guards had descended ahead of him, checked over his shoulder once more, then grabbed the man around the neck with his left arm and applied viselike pressure, cutting off his air. The German tried to yell but couldn't get enough wind to do so. Gideon reached around to his haversack, felt for his grenades, and pulled the strings on two. He pushed the living human bomb off the lip into the gaping cavity of the elevator shaft. The man screamed, plummeting. Then he detonated.

Gideon looked over the edge. The Germans had strung an emergency light from a broken dangling piece of cable to illuminate the way down. The shaft was made of riveted steel, like the inside hull of a U-boat. At the far bottom, sprawled on top of the smashed elevator roof, were the bodies of five soldiers.

He reached to his left, grabbed a seam in the steel with his fingertips, and, using it to keep his balance, walked along the narrow ledge on the inside front wall that led to ladder rungs welded to the side wall. The Germans had designed this bunker well, allowing for emergencies, even providing an emergency ladder in the elevator shaft.

He descended quickly, two rungs at a time, occasionally glancing up to check for new arrivals. When he was about two-thirds of the long way down, he saw a guard enter. By the time he reached the top of the elevator car, there were three soldiers in the shaft with him. Stepping over and around the contorted bodies, he moved to the opposite side of the elevator roof, unstrapped the MP40, planted his feet, waited until the three Germans were a little closer, then opened fire. The enemy soldiers had two options—fumble for their weapons with one hand while holding on with the other, or scoot back up the ladder out of Gideon's range. Neither worked. Struck by Gideon's bullets, the three men plunged down the shaft, crashing a few feet from him.

Working quickly, Gideon pushed bodies aside to clear the hatch in the elevator roof that led inside. While sliding through, he had to avoid a ragged edge of steel shaped by the limpet blast. Then he let go and dropped to a flat area on the mangled, demolished floor.

Now to find Phoenix. He stepped out into the lower passageway.

He didn't like what he saw. Down the hall, German soldiers were congregated outside what he guessed to be the machine-shop door. At worst, that meant Phoenix was trapped inside. At best, it meant that his fellow commandoes had made it to the fuel-storage vault and had blocked off both routes.

Gideon checked his watch. Twenty-seven minutes had passed inside the bunker. There were only eighteen to go.

He ran down the long passageway. Some of the Germans looked toward him, but then turned back to the job at hand—

breaking through the machine-shop door. As far as they were concerned, Gideon was just another Waffen SS guard, coming to help.

He counted fourteen soldiers, plus one man in civilian work clothes who was using an acetylene torch to cut a hole through the metal door.

As he ran down the hallway, Gideon searched the corpses strewn on the ground for grenades. Spotting two sticking from a dead man's jackboots, he bent down to collect them and continued to move.

One of the guards scrutinized him as he approached. Gideon pulled up and checked progress. The workman was almost all the way through.

"The launch vault," Gideon muttered to himself in German, moving through the group.

He walked about thirty feet past the men, activated the grenades, and whirled suddenly to throw them, tossing them low along the floor. He then whipped his gun into firing position and let loose, raking the width of the hall twice. The grenade exploded, sending deadly shrapnel outward. Gideon continued shooting until all movement had ceased.

He ran for the sliced door.

"In'Hout!" he yelled through the cut.

It was El-Said who answered. "We're trapped in here!"

"I've cleaned them out. Come on!"

There were more shouts inside. Gideon flattened against the wall and looked up and down the hall. No guards in sight. He heard the team gathering to push away their barricade. The door opened, and Gideon counted as his comrades and Horvath rushed through. After all six of them emerged, he exhaled in relief.

"Did you get Ulmer?" Kinelly asked.

Gideon shook his head grimly. "He fled."

"The enemy holds the rocket-assembly room," In'Hout reported.

"We'll go around behind them through the launch vault."

"Gideon! Guards!" Said was already positioning his rifle

as the two men who had appeared from the elevator shaft ran toward them.

"Take them," Gideon ordered. The Bedouin cocked his bolt-action Reveilli, crouched down to one knee, aimed, and triggered four quick shots. The Germans pitched forward on their faces.

"Good. Here, give me your pack." Gideon took the heavy rucksack loaded with limpets from Said and strapped it on his own back. "You'll stay in the passageway and guard our rear. Work your way toward the launch-vault doors. Be ready to make a break for the crane when we shout."

Gideon started off with the others.

"What about the emergency shaft?" In'Hout asked, running alongside him.

"Impassable. I dropped a limpet in it from above."

"So that was your doing. When we heard it, we thought maybe the krauts had brought in explosives to blow our barricade."

Gideon stopped suddenly as he drew even with the emergency shaft door. He grabbed In'Hout's arm to stop him as well. "Let's make absolutely certain the shaft remains impassable for a while longer. Get ready to pull open the door."

Gideon drew a limpet from his pack, set the timer, and stood flat against the wall next to the shaft's entrance. He nodded to In'Hout. The Dutchman cracked the door wide enough for Gideon to throw in the explosive, then slammed it shut. As the two men sprinted down the hall after the others, the limpet detonated, the crashing sound of the blast hurting their ears.

"Okay, let's do it!" Gideon shouted. "We'll fight our way to the fuel-storage vault, plant those charges, and get the hell out of here. We've got thirteen minutes."

CHAPTER ELEVEN

"GRENADES READY," GIDEON ordered in a sharp-edged voice. "If there's no return fire, we rush the vault. In two groups. Kinelly and Eliska, you come with me counterclockwise around the pad. Horvath, you go clockwise with Charvey and In'Hout. Each group will have two rucksacks with limpet mines. Whoever reaches the fuel vaults first, start planting the explosives. The trailing group should leave a man to guard the door to the west passageway."

He saw grim, determined nods.

"Okay, hit the switch."

Tibor Horvath obeyed and the doors slid open. As Gideon had expected, there were Germans on the other side—four of them. But Phoenix had the jump, and the Nazis had no time to fire before the grenades bounced at their feet and exploded, ripping them apart.

"Let's go," Gideon shouted.

Phoenix fanned out into two groups around the empty launch pad, one group taking the long way while Gideon dashed toward the cover provided by the pillbox control room that jutted out into the walkway between the two sets of sliding doors.

They made it with no time to spare. A soldier rounded the corner of the squat structure, triggering a burst from his machine pistol. The three Phoenix members flattened against the wall and the bullets flew wide. Before the Nazi could correct his aim, Eliska responded with her Sten, stitching a seam of blood across his chest and spinning him sideways. He crashed to the floor, dead.

Gideon believed there were more Germans on the other side of the control room, guarding the other door. "Grenades," he told Kinelly.

The Irishman swung his Sten over his shoulder, grabbed two grenades off his belt, pulled their pins with his teeth, and flung them over the roof.

They clanged on the metal walkway, then exploded.

Gideon ran around the corner of the control room. To his surprise, a guard with a mutilated, bloody arm was approaching.

Gideon barreled into the German and slammed the barrel of his own MP40 into the man's face. The soldier fell backward onto the floor, and Gideon finished him off at point-blank range.

Kinelly ran past Gideon, raking the walkway in front of the control room. Then Charvey and In'Hout joined the fighting from the other direction, catching the remaining guards in a crossfire.

In a moment, everyone stood before the huge sliding doors leading to the west passageway. The Germans had closed the doors to both passageways, working to the Phoenix team's advantage, enabling them to advance stage by stage toward the fuel vault without alerting the Germans immediately.

They paused to reload their weapons and took grenades in hand. Gideon pulled a limpet from his pack and set the timer to five seconds, holding the clockwork attached to the half-moon casing well away from himself, to be certain not to hit the activating button accidentally. Horvath bent down and retrieved an MP40 dropped by a German. Eliska showed him how to cock it.

"Let's hope whoever's on the other side thinks we're friends," Gideon said.

Kinelly nodded. Then he pounded on the tempered steel with the butt of his Sten. They waited what seemed like an eternity. Kinelly pounded again, and Gideon shouted in German a stern command to open the door. But the barriers didn't move.

"Let's blow it open!" Charvey said impatiently.

"If we have to," Gideon replied bitterly. "But it's going to take a goddam lot of our limpets."

Suddenly, they heard the whirring of an electric motor, and the doors started to part.

"Get back!" Gideon shouted, activating the limpet and lobbing it through the opening.

The other Phoenix members flung their grenades, jumped back from the doorway, and pressed against the walls of the vault.

The passageway erupted in a series of explosions. One man who survived the initial blasts screamed in agony as the thermite incendiary seared his skin. Kinelly, leveling his Sten, stepped into the doorway and silenced the man.

They looked down the passageway for other soldiers. A massive shape pointed at them from the other end—the next test rocket mounted horizontally on its dolly, waiting to be rolled along the tracks into the launch vault. There were no soldiers in sight, but Gideon knew they might be hiding in the shadows.

"Stay here and guard the rear," Gideon told Eliska, who carried no limpets. "Anyone who needs more grenades take them from Eliska's pack—"

There were shots and a grenade blast from behind them. They heard footsteps running along the walkway. In'Hout ran out to look past the control room that blocked their view.

"It's Said," he yelled.

The Bedouin ran up. "There're too many," he said, panting. "I can't hold them off any longer. They started pouring out of the machine shop and the elevator shaft. They must have broken through."

"Quick," Gideon ordered. "Everyone through here. We'll close these doors. They can't be opened from the launch vault." He waited until the others had crossed into the passageway, then closed the doors behind them. "The krauts are following us in a big circle. Round and round we all go."

"How are we going to get out?" Eliska asked. "We just sealed off our escape route."

"There's no choice. We'll have to improvise."

Gideon checked his watch, calculating. Only seven minutes left to the deadline he'd set outside the bunker. Enough time to plant the limpets, possibly, but not enough to escape as well.

Gideon decided to take more time, gambling that Brusilov could continue to hold off the Germans on the surface, above the launch doors.

"We'll set the limpets to detonate at four a.m.," he said. "That'll give us extra time to find an alternate route."

He broke into a run along the tracks, the others behind him. The door they sought stood directly opposite the assembly room on the far side of the rocket that now filled the passageway. As they reached the nose of the monstrous rocket and headed to the left, they heard the sound of boots on concrete to their right.

Gideon squatted. He could see the legs of troops running past. Grenades protruded from shiny jackboots. The leading man would round the rocket's nose in seconds.

Gideon sprayed half a clip under the rocket, chopping the legs out from under the Germans. Soldiers crashed to the floor with shouts of pain and fury. Bullets ripped into heads and bodies as the other Phoenix members opened up.

Gideon tossed his MP40 and two magazines to Said. "Use this instead of the Reveilli." Turning to Eliska, he added, "Use your grenades if more come."

Horvath had already reached the fuel vault's door and was spinning out the combination on its big dials. The tumblers clicked into place. Charvey helped the Hungarian swing open the massive steel slab.

They rushed inside. Horvath clicked on the light. A round steel tank loomed overhead in the first of the five thick-walled compartments. Around the walls were stacked 55-gallon drums of chemical additives used to create the rocket fuel. Their task was to plant six limpets on the large tank in each room, and single mines on the 55-gallon drums.

While Kinelly, Charvey, and Horvath moved on to other rooms, Gideon started setting his remaining limpets. As he went about the mechanical task, an escape plan suddenly came to him—a way to stall the Germans long enough to get the team back to the launch vault and ascend the crane to the surface.

He finished mining the tank in his assigned chamber, then ran toward the only complete XX rocket, where he planted two mines on its nose and two on its fuel-storage compartment.

The clatter of automatic-weapon fire caught his attention. He ran to Eliska, who was crouched, firing toward the door.

"How are you holding out?" he asked.

"They're regrouping in the assembly room."

"I'll stall them," Gideon said. He took a limpet from his pack, turned the fuse to the five-second grenade position, and waited.

Less than a minute later ten Waffen SS troops stormed out of the assembly room. Gideon tossed the limpet, then dove for cover.

The explosion was deafening. Again, he heard the screams of burning men and smelled the nauseating stench of seared flesh.

That would buy some time.

Gideon returned to the fuel vault, ready to implement his escape plan.

He turned left into the first compartment. Metal lockers lined one wall. He opened three before he found the gas masks. Grabbing seven, Gideon tossed them in a pile.

Moving from chamber to chamber he inspected the chemical drums. He found what he wanted in the third room—hydrogen sulfide. He dashed back to retrieve a large dolly and rolled it to a drum of the highly toxic liquid. Straining, he jerked the barrel up and down, tipping it until it stood on the base of the dolly. Then he pushed it through the two outer compartments to the passageway.

He rushed back for another drum. By this time, the others were finished planting their explosives, and Charvey helped Gideon.

"Keep moving toward the launch vault," Gideon instructed the Frenchman. "Someone pass around these masks and someone grab two of the limpets. I'll take the others."

He hurriedly planted his limpets on the first drum he had moved, setting the fuses at three minutes. In'Hout and Kinelly closed the vault door behind them, then passed around the masks.

"Shoot off the lock!" Gideon ordered. He took Horvath's two limpets and set off down the hall after Charvey.

While Eliska and El-Said covered him, guarding the door to the assembly room, Kinelly blasted the dials with a burst from his Sten. There was no way now the Germans could remove the charges in time. Then the three dashed down the tracks.

When they reached the launch-vault doors, Gideon and Charvey pushed the barrel off the dolly onto its side. The sound of automatic weapons again filled the passageway as Kinelly and Eliska fought off two charging soldiers.

"Put on your masks!" Gideon slapped the last two limpets onto the ends of the barrel and set the clocks for forty-five seconds.

They adjusted their gas masks. Said tossed Gideon his MP40, cocking his own Reveilli and taking two grenades in hand.

"Horvath, get ready to open the doors," Gideon said, pushing his mask aside. "In'Hout and Charvey, get a leg on the barrel. As soon as the doors open, push hard. You others cover us. Everyone be ready to jump back. Horvath, when we can advance, go to the control room and open the launch doors. Charvey, get on the crane and raise the boom. The rest of us will climb it. Okay, let's go." He looked at his watch, starting the countdown. "Ten seconds . . . five . . . now!"

Horvath hit the switch, and the doors parted. Said lobbed his grenades. Eliska and Kinelly raked the walkway with their Stens. The three men on the drum pushed with their legs. It rolled into the launch vault. A German seemed to part in midair as the grenades exploded. Others dove for the walkway to shoot back.

"Duck!" Gideon bellowed, his cry muffled through the mask.

The two explosions, behind and in front of them, were just a split-second out of synchronization. The barrels split open and the hydrogen sulfide spilled out, burning like lava. Caustic, noxious fumes filled the bunker. The Germans stumbled past one another on the walkway, crowding toward the east passageway in search of fresh air. One man, splashed in the face with the chemical, held his eyes, screaming. Eliska finished him with a quick burst.

Phoenix, avoiding the smoldering chemical mire, entered the launch vault. Charvey raked the retreating soldiers. Kinelly guarded the rear. The west passageway along the tracks was filled with flames and fumes, securing that route and prohibiting the Germans from gaining access to the launch vault.

Gideon checked his watch. They had just over five minutes to get out of the bunker and get far enough away to avoid the coming conflagration.

He ran toward the control room with Horvath; it had occurred to him that there might be Germans still inside who would overpower the Hungarian. It was empty. Gideon waited until he was certain the doors were operational. Horvath fiddled at the control panel a moment, then gave him the thumbs-up sign. In response, Gideon pointed to his watch and held up two fingers. Horvath nodded sharply, the insect-like gas mask jerking up and down. Gideon took off.

He had planned to assume a position at the doorway to the east passageway to cover the escape, but Kinelly was already there, his Sten ready. The guards probably would have retreated to get gas masks, then would return in force.

The desert floor outside the launch doors was the other critical point. What they'd run into above depended on Brusilov, and Gideon trusted that the Russian would hold his position at all costs, even if the time deadline had passed.

He reached the crane. Charvey was already in the cab, skillfully maneuvering the boom to the top of the vault, just under the doors. He found the location he wanted and extended the boom to one end of the middle seam. That way, the Phoenix team could begin to climb out before the doors were completely open.

The moment the Frenchman locked the crane in place, Eliska began the precarious ascent up the tall, latticed steel. She gripped the boom as she moved upward, two cross supports at a time. In'Hout followed, then Said, Charvey, and Gideon. In the control room, Horvath pressed the button to open the launch doors, threw the backup locking switch, and ran to join the others as the electric motor clicked to life.

The ceiling of the vault rumbled open, exposing the dark sky. Fresh air streamed into the bunker as smoke and fumes rose out. Those high on the boom ripped off their masks, making the climb easier.

Eliska stumbled and slammed flat against the face of the boom, banging into the cross supports. Behind her, Gideon quickly grabbed her thighs, holding her in place until she regained her grip. Above them, they saw In'Hout scramble off the top of the boom, over the steel-girder doorframe, and out on to the sand. The edge of the doors clanged against the stops and the growling motor died.

Gideon's mind ticked off the moments that determined life or death. He climbed on.

Gunshots rang out from below, and Horvath started up the boom. Kinelly was on the top of the cab, firing at soldiers in gas masks charging through both doors. He raked one group, then another. When the Sten clicked empty, he abandoned it, then turned to climb.

Said had reached the top. Eliska, Gideon, and Charvey followed, jumping from the crown of the boom, over the edge of the frame, and onto the desert floor. In'Hout unloaded his grenades. They banged onto the walkway and exploded in the midst of Germans. Said scanned the night for movement as Eliska and Gideon fired into the vault.

The soldiers fired on Kinelly and Horvath. Charvey reached down to help pull the Hungarian over the edge.

Horvath had made it. But below him, Kinelly was caught in a crossfire, slugs ripping into his body.

His feet slipped out from under him and his legs dangled.

Flinging both arms over a crossbar, he managed to hold on despite his wounds. Several Germans started up the boom after him while others emerged from the passageways below, braving the Phoenix fire.

Another shot slammed into Kinelly. The others watched from above as a soldier came up behind him. The Irishman held on with one arm as he reached to his belt and pulled the pins on his last three grenades. He took three men with him as he toppled in the violent explosion.

For a moment there was a stunned silence.

"He told me to go first. He saved my life. That should have been me!"

Horvath's hoarse whisper snapped Gideon back into action. He looked at his watch. Seconds left.

"Come on! Come on!" he screamed. As they headed west toward open desert, they found Brusilov waiting at the southern slope of the escarpment, his Bren held ready. He dropped the gun and joined them in their desperate run over the soft desert sand.

When the explosion came, the *Betonunterstand* erupted like a volcano. First there was a powerful roar from the bowels of the earth, shaking the ground.

Then the top blew.

The runners were knocked down by the tremendous force of the blast. Dazed and spent, they lay motionless as the giant fire burned behind them.

CHAPTER TWELVE

FROM THE SOUTH came the sound of numerous secondary explosions, and in the brief orange flashes of light, they could see huge, inky torrents of smoke pouring upward into the night. The desert breeze carried the pungent, acrid stench of burning petrol, rubber, chemicals, and flesh.

A new urgency drove Gideon as he led the others across the sand. Ulmer had escaped. They had to stop him from getting to Germany, and their only hope was the airplane that would be waiting for them on the desert at dawn, a little less than an hour and a half from now. Their mission would be a failure if they didn't make it in time.

Gideon fought against the deep pain of Kinelly's death as he forced himself to move at top speed. Other Phoenix members had fallen, but each death hit him as badly as the first. Kinelly's was especially hard to take. The irascible ex-sailor's unquenchable spirit had lifted them in many tight spots. He had been with the team since its formation in 1939, when Gideon had led Phoenix across the Belgian-German border for the long trek to Poland on their first mission.

Grief showed plainly on the faces of the others; Brusilov had noted Kinelly's absence and read the Irishman's fate from the expressions of his comrades. But Gideon knew that once they reached the camp, the team would again focus entirely on the mission still before them.

"How much farther?" he finally gasped to Said.

"The other side of the large dune ahead. We're almost—" The Bedouin stopped abruptly and stood still, listening.

"What is it?" Gideon demanded. Then he heard the faint, eerie cry wafting on the wind.

"Hurry!" Said shouted, breaking again into a run.

The team raced after him as he climbed the dune. He halted at the top, listening.

Over the sound of his own panting, Gideon clearly heard the awful agonized sounds of wounded camels below, as the desert breeze carried forth the familiar smell of cordite and death.

"Sale con," Charvey swore under his breath. *"Un massacre."*

"An ambush?" Eliska asked.

"No," Gideon replied. "They would have waited for us." He paused for a moment, then called out, "Brusilov, In'Hout, circle wide to the left. Eliska and Charvey, to the right. Watch for tracks."

They moved off. Gideon, with Said and Horvath, headed directly for their campsite.

The expanse of sand below was littered with the bodies of dead and dying animals, their pale-pink *azrem* soaked with blood. The fusilade of bullets had been so intense that all the water jugs were punctured, the radio and tents destroyed, and the one pack of extra ammunition detonated. Some food was salvageable, but the only water they had now was what little remained in their canteens.

Brusilov approached Gideon. "German patrol tracks. They were in a half-track, and must have used the machine gun to do this damage."

Gideon grimaced. Eliska joined them, bringing no new information. "Any sign of Masucci?" she asked.

Gideon shook his head. "I never should have brought that traitor along. It was an unnecessary risk."

"Although we are fighting the Nazis, we must not allow ourselves to become like them," Said commented. "Saving the Italian was the humane thing to do. There is no evidence that he betrayed us."

"There's no evidence he didn't," Gideon said. Turning to Eliska, he ordered, "Get the others over here."

Said watched her go. "What is your plan?"

"I'm not sure. We can't make the rendezvous point in time on foot?"

The Bedouin shook his head.

Gideon continued. "We can't catch Ulmer on foot either. And we can't stay here—the Germans will be swarming over the area searching for us."

He stood, thinking, as the rest of the Phoenix team gathered. "We're going to move out immediately. South, toward the landing site."

"But surely we can't make it on time?" Brusilov asked him.

"No. But our only hope of catching up with Ulmer, slim as it is, depends on the plane. I'm gambling that our pilot may spot us on his way into or out of the rendezvous point. Besides," he added, "with our camels dead and our supplies gone, the Germans will expect us to move north, toward the coast, not deeper into the desert."

They stood in silence for a moment. Then Charvey said, "I cannot believe that as a boy I would have done anything to go to the beach and play in the sand. Now I would rather take on a battalion of Boches than bear that desert sun."

The Frenchman's remark broke the tension. "Let's get moving," Gideon ordered.

They set off at a brisk pace, Said leading the way. After half an hour, the sky began lightening slowly from black to a pale gray to pink. As he marched, Gideon's head was craned upward, searching for the black speck of a plane. But he saw nothing.

Another hour passed. As the yellow sun climbed above the horizon into the slate-blue sky, Said called a halt.

"We are roughly in the flight path the plane should follow to return to Egypt. We might as well stay here."

Gideon nodded. He ordered the others to stay close, making the group more visible from the air.

Each minute seemed like ten as they waited. Even in the morning coolness, the slogging through the sand had made them red-faced and sweat-soaked. They knew that the sun would soon turn the sky from blue to white, and by nine a.m., the heat would be unbearable.

Another half hour passed. Gideon was about to talk to Said about an alternative plan when In'Hout shouted, "A plane!"

It took Gideon a moment to spot the moving black speck. Then he heard the faint whine of engines and caught a brief flash of sun reflecting off metal.

The members of the Phoenix team started waving their arms. Gideon stood still. Something wasn't quite right.

Then it dawned on him. The plane was coming from the north, not from the rendezvous spot to the south. As the aircraft descended toward them, he saw that it was a fighter, not a transport.

"Scatter!" Gideon yelled.

The Phoenix team sprinted in different directions, then hit the sand as the plane swooped in. Bullets kicked up in a double row. As the fusillade stopped, Brusilov and Charvey jumped up and fired at the aircraft, but their bullets sailed uselessly in open sky.

Gideon saw that the aircraft was an Italian Fiat G.50 Freccia, an all-metal single-seat fighter armed with two 12.7mm machine guns. With its 840-horsepower engine, the Freccia was much faster than the Gibli reconnaissance plane he and In'Hout had shot down on their way to the bunker. The chance of shooting down the fighter with their submachine guns was very slim.

The Freccia had completed its turn and was roaring toward them again. Gideon could think of only one option.

"Charvey, In'Hout, Horvath. Sprawl out and play dead! The rest of you, follow me. When the firing starts, pretend you're hit!"

He stood up and ran toward the open desert, far enough away from Charvey, In'Hout, and Horvath so that the plane wouldn't strafe them again. He heard Said, Eliska, and Brusilov running after him.

The escalating whine told him the Freccia was angling behind him for the kill. Then the machine gun opened up, sending sand flying.

Out of the corner of his eye, Gideon saw Eliska suddenly throw up her arms. Her Sten gun flew away from her and she toppled into the sand. Behind her, Brusilov pitched forward, his big body somersaulting as it hit the ground. Said tumbled left, falling on his back with arms splayed.

Only Gideon was standing when the plane pulled out from its second pass. He fired a burst from his MP40 as the fighter soared upward.

"Don't move!" Gideon shouted over the noise of the plane.

He watched the Freccia bank and turn, estimating its angle of approach on its next pass. Then he began to sprint, leading the plane away from the others.

It seemed like an eternity until the machine guns began to chatter. He took a quick glance over his shoulder and saw two lines of splashing sand pointed directly at him. Despite the desert heat, he felt a sudden chill course through him, like icy water forced through his veins.

But the two lines passed on either side of him. Gideon watched the Freccia roar past, then fired off a complete clip to let the pilot know he was still alive.

With each pass, Gideon's risk of being hit multiplied. But with each pass, he drew the Italian fighter farther away from the others.

The plane dove again, sending out a blistering hail of lead. This time Gideon doubled up, then tumbled backward head over heels, his weapon flying. The fall stunned him, and for a long moment he didn't know whether or not he'd really been hit.

As he lay motionless, he heard the noise of the Freccia's single engine fading.

But soon the noise began to grow again. Gideon's heart dropped. The plane was coming in to strafe the bodies, to make sure everyone was dead.

The sound of the engine seemed to fade again. For a moment Gideon couldn't believe his ears. He lay still, barely breathing, expecting the machine guns to spit death once more.

From the distance, a voice called, "Gideon!"

He jumped to his feet to see Eliska waving at him. Forcing thoughts of the plane from his mind, he ran toward her.

"Said's been hit!" she shouted.

In'Hout, the team's medic, reached the Bedouin at the same time as Gideon. Blood was pouring from Said's shoulder, and his breathing was heavy and labored. His eyes fluttered open as Eliska raised a canteen to his lips.

"*Bismallah,*" he managed to say.

"Stay quiet," In'Hout instructed, taking over. The Dutchman started cutting away the layers of clothing to inspect the wound.

Gideon sighed as he watched. Said was the one person they couldn't afford to lose, not with a hundred miles of desert to cross on foot.

"What do you think?" Gideon asked.

In'Hout didn't reply immediately. His fingers probed flesh. Then he said, "The bullet passed through without hitting bone. He'll be all right, but he's lost a lot of blood. I'm afraid he might go into shock if we move him right away."

Gideon grimaced. They had to get moving. The Freccia had no doubt radioed their position to headquarters. They'd barely survived the encounter with a single aircraft. On foot in open desert, they'd never escape a squadron of fighters or a motorized patrol.

"Do the best you can," Gideon said to In'Hout. "I'll give you a couple of minutes to get him ready to travel."

He stood, thinking. Without the Bedouin's guidance, he had no idea which way to go. North, toward the coast, was the obvious direction. But they'd never make it unless they got to an oasis soon to replenish their food and water supplies.

In his concentration, Gideon didn't hear Brusilov approach,

but turning, he saw the concerned look on the Russian's broad face.

"What's wrong?" Gideon asked, getting to his feet.

"I know why the Italian fighter flew off," Brusilov said. "Look." He pointed to the south.

Gideon's eyes followed. At first he didn't know what he was looking at. A solid wall of yellow brick seemed to have been erected in the middle of the desert. An instant later, the wall seemed to crumble as it moved toward them.

"Sandstorm!" Gideon exclaimed. "Shit!"

He'd been warned about these immense hurricanes hundreds of feet high and more than a mile long, driven by gale-force winds, storms that had buried entire villages under tons of sand.

Gideon scanned the landscape for shelter, but there wasn't a rock in sight. The best they could do would be to try to reach the downwind side of the nearest big dune, to the north.

"Run!" Gideon yelled above the hiss of the wind.

He looked to his left. Brusilov was lifting the injured Said. Gideon paused to help Horvath, who was exhausted and limping. They lagged behind the others, barely visible in the already blinding, swirling light dust. In moments, Gideon knew the heavier, coarser sand in the heart of the storm would overwhelm them.

They crested a smaller dune. For an instant, Gideon considered stopping, but decided to push on. The taller one ahead was far less likely to flatten out in a raging storm.

By the time he reached the base of the whaleback dune, the storm was so intense he could see no one but Horvath, whose arm he held. They started to climb, the soft sand slipping out from under their hands and feet, pulling them down half a foot for every forward step. Horvath fell twice, and each time Gideon pushed his strength to the limit to drag the Hungarian to his feet.

They reached the top as the front edge of the heavy sand slammed into them. Gideon and Horvath lost their footing, tumbling down the far side. As he rolled, Gideon got a brief glimpse of Eliska and Charvey before he pulled his hood over his head.

The wind was now a deafening roar, the sand a churning mass. Catching a breath of air was nearly impossible, and Gideon found himself coughing and wheezing. Occasionally the violent whirlpool would intensify enough to slap Gideon to the ground, forcing him to rise to prevent being buried in the sand.

The storm seemed to rage on for an eternity. Gideon couldn't see more than a few inches from his face, and he had no way of telling how the rest of the team was faring. He tried to rise to his knees and crawl around to check, but the rough-edged wind bowled him over. All they could do was wait.

Finally, the tumult abated, the heavy wall of sand moving north toward the Mediterranean. Slowly Gideon cleared off the sand, got to his feet, and searched for his comrades.

The others had survived. One by one, they rose, nodding to Gideon or clasping his hand as he reached them. They didn't speak, their mouths and noses dry from the sand, their lungs aching. Gideon found a canteen, and they passed it around, taking small sips of the precious liquid.

Gideon turned his attention to Said. Brusilov had sheltered the wounded Bedouin, constantly clearing sand from his face. He was semiconscious, but his breathing was regular and his heart still strong.

"Can he travel?" Gideon asked In'Hout.

The Dutchman shrugged. "I guess we don't have much choice."

Gideon surveyed the desert around them. Erratic dust-laden gusts still swirled like small whirlwinds, and the sun above was a dim globe through the thick haze. The visibility was still poor enough to keep the German aircraft on the ground awhile longer, he thought. That gave them some precious time to put distance between themselves and the ruins of the bunker.

"Which way are we heading?" Brusilov asked.

"North," Gideon replied. "I got a compass reading on

Ulmer's track. Without Said's guidance, our only real choice is to follow that heading."

"We might run into a German patrol," the Russian said.

"I hope we do."

"Why?"

"They'd have water," Gideon said. He looked up at the blazing sun. "For once, the Nazis aren't our worst enemy."

CHAPTER THIRTEEN

THE GRITTY WIND gradually abated, and the sky turned from yellow to white. The sun beat down on them unmercifully as they slogged through the soft, shifting sands. As the day wore on, the symptoms of dehydration set in—intense thirst, fever, nausea, an overwhelming sleepiness. Tibor Horvath, who lacked the physical conditioning of the Phoenix team, suffered the worst. Brusilov carried Said, with occasional relief from the others.

Every hour Gideon paused for a short rest, trying to find a spot of shade under the slipface of a dune. A canteen was passed around, with each person permitted two small sips.

Said had said that the Bedouin way was to drink only three times a day—morning, noon, and night. Now Gideon knew why. They were all obsessed by water, and taking only a sip when their minds and bodies ached for more was as horrible a torture as their sun-parched skin. Only the mental toughness that drove them to complete each impossible mission compelled the team onward.

Finally, the sun dipped below the horizon. Darkness came suddenly, as if a lamp had been extinguished, and with the blackness came extraordinary relief from the intense heat.

But there was no relief from the thirst. Gideon called a halt, and they passed around the last canteen, finishing off all but a few swallows of their water. They fell to the sand, totally exhausted.

The sandstorm had prevented them from salvaging any

food. Although dehydration had taken away their appetite, they hadn't eaten in over twenty-four hours. Gideon knew their energy reserves had to be nearly depleted.

He lay back for a few minutes, thinking, then got to his feet and joined Brusilov.

"How many weapons did we save after the storm?" he asked.

"Three," Brusilov replied. "Two submachine guns and a pistol."

"Ammunition?"

"Ten clips for the MP40s. Only one for the Walther." The Russian looked at Gideon for a moment, then asked, "What do you have in mind?"

"Horvath can't move another step, and without rest, Said will die. If we don't get water and food, tomorrow's sunrise will be our last. Our only chance is to scout as much territory as we can. You, Charvey, and I will take the weapons and follow the desert track the Germans took."

Brusilov grimaced and turned away, gazing out toward the vastness of the Sahara. He spoke without looking at Gideon. "After the revolution, the Red Army drove us thousands of miles over the Siberian plains. How I survived the cold and hunger, I do not know."

He paused for a moment, then added, "But I swore then on the grave of my mother I would not die without a weapon in my hand and Bolsheviks falling around me. Now, it seems to me that when the sun rises again, my throat will be so parched I won't even be able to curse the Communists before I die."

Gideon put his hand on the Russian's shoulder. "We will find water," he said. "Let's go."

Charvey dropped out after an hour, the victim of intense stomach cramps that made it impossible for him to keep up. Gideon gave him one of the two compasses and told him to rest, then make his way back to the others.

Gideon and Brusilov pushed on. Their minds numbed by

exhaustion, they forced themselves to trudge painfully toward a horizon that seemed a million miles away. They moved hour after hour with no rest, the agony of getting to their feet again not worth the brief respite. As midnight approached, they walked as if in a trance.

When Brusilov spoke, it was as startling as a shout. "Look."

"What is it?"

Brusilov pointed.

At first Gideon thought the Russian was calling his attention to a low-hanging star. Slowly he realized the flickering light was too large and too intense. When the light disappeared for a moment, a jolt ran through Gideon—a man had crossed in front of a fire.

Suddenly, Gideon's exhaustion lifted. Without a word, he and Brusilov started forward.

They moved down a large dune, across a flat of harder sand, then up another steep rise, approaching the top cautiously, weapons ready, even though their silhouettes would be hard to see against the black sky.

Gideon broke the dune's plane first, lifting his head. His first reaction was to smile, despite the pain in his cracked lips.

Beside him, he heard Brusilov grunt with satisfaction. They both stared in disbelief at the small German convoy camped for the night.

Below, five hundred meters away, six vehicles had been pulled into a rough circle—a command car, four armored personnel carriers, and a small half-track with a .50-caliber machine gun mounted in the rear. Four rows of tents were set up beyond the parked vehicles, and a handful of men sat around a fire in the center of the circle.

"The Germans are overconfident," Brusilov whispered to Gideon.

"They control this area completely," Gideon said. "British air patrols would concentrate on the roads near the coast, where Rommel's forces are massing."

"They're on their way to the bunker?"

"Probably," Gideon said. He stared down for a moment, then asked, "How many men, do you think?"

"From the number of tents, I would say a hundred." He turned to Gideon and added, "A hundred against two. We can steal the food and water we need."

Gideon shook his head. "With our weapons, we'd be able to carry only one ten-liter can each. That's barely a day's supply—tomorrow we'd be back in the same boat. Besides, we've got to get to the coast and stop Ulmer. We need transportation."

"They'd be after us in no time," Brusilov said. "And they'd radio for Luftwaffe fighters."

"I know," Gideon replied. "That's why we've got to get all of them."

Brusilov raised an eyebrow. "I think the sun has baked your brain."

Gideon smiled. "Maybe. But I have a plan. Have you seen any American western movies?"

"A few."

"We're going to play Indian," Gideon said. "And that wagon train will be our target."

The Wehrmacht sentry was rounding the rear of the armored personnel carrier when he heard a noise. He stopped and started to turn. A huge hand slapped across his mouth and yanked back his head. He started to struggle, then a knife was plunged into the side of his neck, ripping out his windpipe and severing his carotid arteries. The soldier spasmed once, then died.

With great care, Brusilov lowered the body to the ground. He tore the canteen from the man's web gear and drained half of it in three large gulps. He passed the canteen to Gideon, who finished it.

They crouched for a moment, listening for movement and savoring their first drink. They heard nothing except the crackle of burning wood and the faint clink of a sergeant cleaning his weapon in the firelight.

Silently, Brusilov lifted the soldier's body and moved toward the desert. Gideon unstrapped a fuel can from the side of the armored personnel carrier and followed.

They halted on the far side of a slight rise, a hundred meters outside the camp, then quickly stripped off the German's uniform.

Gideon emptied two clips of thirty cartridges, stuffing half the shells into the German's tunic pocket, while Brusilov placed the other half into the pants pockets. Then Brusilov soaked the garments in gasoline.

The soldier had been carrying three grenades, which Gideon put into his belt. He stood and whispered, "I'll wait for your signal."

Brusilov nodded and moved to the left. He circled the camp at a distance of a hundred meters, until he was near the tents in which the soldiers slept. He dropped the fuel-soaked tunic, poured a thin ten-meter trail of fuel, dropped the pants, then continued the fuel trail until the can was empty.

He waited a few minutes, giving Gideon time to get into position. Then he lit a match, ignited the end of the fuel trail, and sprinted as far to his left as he could.

Behind him, he heard the sizzling of fire moving along the ground, then the whoosh of the pants igniting. He'd run about thirty meters when the first cartridges went off.

Brusilov dropped to the ground behind a small sand mound a few feet away. He slapped a full clip in his MP40, laid two more in the sand within easy reach, and sighted toward the camp.

The cartridges in the uniform shirt were going off now. Brusilov heard shouting from the tents, and he saw the muzzle flashes as a few Germans began wildly returning fire into the darkness.

Brusilov waited another minute. Then he squeezed the trigger, swinging the barrel of his weapon back and forth as he peppered the tents with three long sustained bursts. The shouts of officers now mixed with screams of pain.

Gideon had moved into the shadow of the armored personnel carrier. He propped the short barrel of his MP40 on the rear bumper and trained it on the back of the German sergeant sitting by the fire.

Suddenly, there came the sound of firing, and the sergeant jumped to his feet. Gideon pulled the trigger. The back of the Nazi's tunic turned crimson and he pitched head-first into the fire.

Gideon hurriedly fused a grenade, tossed it into the cab of the personnel carrier, and began to run. He heard the grenade detonate behind him as he threw a second potato masher into the cab of a second APC. Then he dashed into the open toward the other vehicles parked on the opposite side.

He was halfway across when a submachine gun opened up behind him. Gideon dove to his left and rolled twice as bullets kicked up the dirt behind him. In one swift motion, he came to his knees and triggered a long burst toward the enemy. He had trouble seeing in the darkness, but he heard a scream just before he caught a glimpse of a body tumbling to the ground.

He picked up movement out the corner of his eye and pivoted as two more Germans jumped from the rear of a third truck. Gideon pulled the trigger, but the hammer clicked on an empty chamber. As a fusillade passed over his head, he dropped his machine pistol, pulled out his last grenade, yanked the string, and hurled it under the personnel carrier. He dropped to the ground, hands shielding his head. The grenade exploded, hurling sand and metal fragments through the air. Gideon was about to rise when the fuel tank exploded, and another shrapnel-filled gale blew past him.

Gideon jumped to his feet. While he slapped a fresh clip in his MP40, he scanned the open area.

He couldn't see any Germans. The firing from the area of the tents had intensified. He had a few minutes.

Dashing for the small half-track with the machine gun mounted in back, he leaped into the driver's seat and pressed the starter button. The diesel coughed twice, then died. He punched the button a second time, then a third.

Behind him, Gideon heard shouts as German soldiers retreated toward him. He fought back panic as he stabbed the starter a fifth time.

The engine caught. He stomped on the accelerator, feeding fuel. When the RPMs were high, he depressed the clutch and rammed the gearshift into first.

With a squeal, the half-track shot toward the desert. Gideon accelerated as quickly as he could, seeking the cover of darkness. When he was out of the light of the burning vehicles, he made a hard left and slowed.

He'd traveled a bumpy couple hundred meters when he saw the brief flaring of a match. He yanked the steering wheel right and slowed more. The night was so dark that Brusilov was only a few steps away before Gideon spotted him.

"Good work," Gideon said.

"Let's finish it," the Russian said, climbing into the back of the half-track. He pushed forward the cover catch of the machine gun, lifted the feed cover, laid a cartridge belt in the feedway, then snapped the cover shut.

"Ready!" he shouted to Gideon.

Gideon slipped the clutch and accelerated, driving toward the German camp. When he reached a point about a hundred meters from the tents, he veered right, and Brusilov opened fire, strafing the tents with a deadly fusillade of lead. Sporadic shots passed behind them as Gideon circled the camp. Agonized cries punctuated the staccato crackling of the machine gun.

As Gideon rounded the flaming vehicles, he saw the fourth undamaged APC racing into the desert. Gideon stepped on the accelerator and gave chase. He lost sight of his target for a moment as the personnel carrier topped a small dune. The half-track shot over the top, landing with a jolt that nearly sent Brusilov pitching into the sand.

The personnel carrier was now less than twenty meters in front of them. Soldiers in the rear opened fire with MP40s, but Gideon cut to the left to pass. Despite the bouncing, Brusilov managed to feed a fresh belt into his MG42. As the half-track came even with the cab of the vehicle, Brusilov opened fire.

The glass in the cab shattered as the personnel carrier careened left. Braking hard to avoid a collision, Gideon brought the half-track to a halt and watched the German vehicle hit the side of a steep dune, slow, then tip over.

Brusilov opened fire again as men tried to crawl out from under the vehicle. Germans sprawled over the sand, screaming in pain. Then the screams were lost in the roar of the exploding fuel tank.

Brusilov ceased fire. "Do we make another pass at the camp?" he asked Gideon.

Gideon debated. "No need to waste the fuel. The Germans aren't going anywhere."

Eliska forced herself to fight against sleep throughout the endless night. She heard the others toss and turn in their fitful rest, occasionally moaning or crying out from nightmares caused by hunger and dehydration. To Eliska, the thought of suffering such bad dreams was incentive enough to stay awake.

She also felt a duty to stand guard, even though she could do nothing if attacked. Gideon and Brusilov had taken the weapons, and they were almost too weak to stand, much less fight.

Eliska had faced no other combat situation with the Phoenix team that seemed as desperate as their present plight. They weren't fighting the enemy, but the relentless demands of their own bodies. The thought of the sun rising again was almost unbearable.

A jolt went through her as the desert breeze brought forth the faint sound of a motor. A plane?

Despite her weakness, she managed to get to her feet and shake In'Hout. He muttered, but didn't awaken. She moved to Charvey. The Frenchman sat up, wiping sleep out of his eyes.

He stood next to Eliska, listening as the vehicle approached. "It's a truck of some kind. What do we do?" he asked.

Then the shout came over the roar of the engine. "Wake up!"

Eliska couldn't believe her ears for a moment. A sudden energy went through her as she ran forward, shouting, "Scott! Thank God!"

CHAPTER FOURTEEN

GIDEON OPENED HIS eyes. The sky was light, but the early-morning breeze was still cool. He heard the sounds of cooking to his right, and he started to rise.

He stopped, abruptly. Something was crawling down his right arm. He turned his head. A large, black, crablike insect was on his forearm. Not an insect—a scorpion.

A wave of panic flooded over him. Gideon fought back the nearly overwhelming impulse to jerk his arm away. A scorpion sting might be fatal to him as well as to the mission.

He waited, hoping the arachnid would crawl off him. He breathed slowly, shallowly, silently counting off the seconds. The scorpion moved a few inches, then rested on the back of his hand. Gideon fought off a shudder of disgust.

"Eliska!" he called out. His voice was hoarse from sleep.

He cleared his throat, then called again.

He could hear her approaching. "Scott, what . . ." Her words trailed off in a gasp as she saw the scorpion.

"Use a knife," Gideon said. "Approach it slowly, then flick it away."

She pulled her knife from its sheath. Holding her breath, she inched forward, bent, then with a quick backhand motion slapped the scorpion from Gideon's hand. Gideon jumped up and killed the creature with his boot.

He exhaled a loud sigh of relief. Then he looked at Eliska and said, "I think the scorpion was punishment for catching a couple hours' sleep. We should have moved out before dawn."

"You and Brusilov were exhausted," she replied. "And the rest of us needed the time for the food and water to restore our strength."

"How's Said?" Gideon asked.

"Much better. He's still weak, but he's conscious. I think he can sit up for the drive."

"Good," Gideon said. "Get everyone ready. We've got to get out of this area as fast as we can."

Eliska nodded. Gideon moved over to talk to the Bedouin, who was in an upright position, leaning against the half-track.

Gideon crouched next to him. "The sandstorm obliterated Ulmer's trail. Where do you think he's headed?"

"Northward, there are two major German airfields, Sirte to the west, El Agheila to the east. Sirte is closer, and more removed from the British front lines. There would be less risk of being spotted by enemy aircraft or encountering a Long Range Desert Patrol."

"We've got to assume a man like Ulmer will make the most logical decision," Gideon said. "And that he followed the major German north-south track. But we're likely to be spotted in daylight if we take that route."

"I can direct you another way," Said offered. "It will mean heading farther west at first, but we can make up the time because we will be traveling on harder ground when we turn north."

"We'll do it," Gideon said. "I only wish we knew if Ulmer and his escort were as badly delayed by the sandstorm as we were."

"Only Allah knows that."

Gideon became accustomed to the mirages, the picture-making games the sun played as the light passed through air layers of different temperatures. As the half-track bounced across the rough desert floor, Gideon saw tantalizing shimmering lakes, camel caravans, palm trees, even fantastic war machines that seemed to waddle toward them on stilts.

The mirages were a relief from the nearly unbearable heat. They had water now, but that didn't heal their seriously sunburned skin, badly cracked lips, and swollen tongues. Their condition was such that if the engine beneath the hood of the half-track sputtered to a halt, stranding them in the desert, they would certainly soon die.

But the half-track performed, carrying them north out of the Great Sand Sea. By late afternoon, a yellow wall was growing on the horizon in front of them. Gideon, awaking from a short nap, had feared at first glance another sandstorm was approaching them. Said quickly explained that the wall was the line of cliffs separating the desert from the narrow coastal plain, along which ran the road controlled by Rommel's army.

"How tall are the cliffs?" Gideon asked.

"Several hundred meters," the Bedouin replied.

"How are we going to get this half-track over the top?" In'Hout asked.

"The closest road is thirty kilometers to the east."

"We don't have time for that," Gideon commented. "Sirte is west of here. How far?"

"Twenty kilometers."

"Where is the road?"

"Between the cliffs and the Gulf of Sidra. The coastal plain is very narrow here, perhaps a kilometer wide and very flat. The road is the only fast way to travel."

Gideon remained silent, thinking, as the mountains gradually loomed larger in front of them. When they reached the foothills, he asked Brusilov, "How much fuel do we have left?"

"The tank is almost empty, and we have one jerry can remaining. Enough for thirty or forty kilometers, over this terrain."

"That's it," Gideon said. "Even if we detoured to the road over the mountains, we'd arrive on the other side without fuel."

"We're abandoning this half-track?" Brusilov asked.

"We can't leave it where the Germans might spot it," Gideon said. He turned to Said. "Any suggestions?"

"I have an idea," the Bedouin said.

He directed Brusilov northwest. They rounded an outcropping of rock, then crossed a fissured wadi with ground gradually sloping to a depression Said called a *shabcha*, or dried-up lake. Brusilov maneuvered across the dry, dusty bottom to a narrow gully shadowed by overhanging rock.

"The Germans will not be able to see the vehicle from the air," Said explained. "And there is little chance a ground patrol will venture back this far."

"It's perfect," Gideon said. "There's always the chance we might have to recross the mountains to make our escape after the raid on Sirte."

"Are we climbing now?" In'Hout asked.

Before Gideon could reply, Said suggested, "It would be better to rest until dark, so we do not have to climb in the heat and waste energy. While we wait, we can refresh ourselves. In the wadi, on the top of those small hummocks, grow prickly thorns. Their pulp is very sweet and juicy, like a melon. The desert tribes use it as an important source of energy."

"Sounds good," Gideon said. "Lead the way."

The sky was black and star-laden as they made their way up the rocky slope. The members of the Phoenix team and the Hungarian scientist were stronger than they'd been since the attack on the bunker, and even Said was able to maintain the pace.

Only Gideon's mood was dark, as he thought about the immense difficulties they'd face in completing their mission. According to Said, the coast road was full of military traffic both day and night, and the Germans had set up heavily fortified checkpoints every five to ten kilometers. They'd have to find a way to pass these checkpoints undetected.

If they accomplished that, there remained the airfield at Sirte to penetrate. Defenses at these airfields had been heavily increased since the success of two or three British commando raids earlier in the war. And with an important scientist like Ulmer on the base, the garrison would be on full alert.

If Ulmer was still in North Africa. Nearly forty-eight hours had passed since the bunker had been destroyed, ample time for the scientist to have reached the airfield and boarded a plane for Germany. If that was true, Gideon might be leading Phoenix into a suicide mission conducted in vain.

But he had no choice. His orders were to kill Ulmer and destroy the rocket plans at any cost.

They climbed for two hours before they reached a pass between wind-sculpted fists of rock that opened a view to the narrow, dark expanse of land between the mountains and the shimmering mass of the Mediterranean. Gideon knelt, hand on his chin, staring down at a black ribbon winding through the middle of the plain—the coastal road. To the east, Gideon could see a line of headlights moving slowly westward.

Brusilov knelt beside him. "What is your plan?"

Gideon continued to stare into the night. Then he turned to Brusilov. "I'm not sure," he admitted. "That road is crawling with German vehicles and checkpoints, and we've got to travel twenty kilometers to Sirte. Do you have an idea?"

Brusilov pointed to the east. "Those lights. From the way they're moving, they must be tanks. Horvath, Said, and Eliska could be concealed inside a tank, out of sight of checkpoint guards. A desert tank commander might well have a sunburn like yours. And if we do get to Sirte, we will have the firepower to attack the airfield."

"A tank would be perfect. But our chances of taking one without attracting attention are very slim."

Brusilov smiled. "Our chances of survival aren't good anyway. If we're going to die, why not sooner than later?"

Gideon returned the smile. "Why not? Let's get down to the road."

The descent took over an hour, during which the tank convoy passed. While the others waited in the rocks at the base of the coastal heights, Gideon led Brusilov and In'Hout to an observation point near a bend in the highway.

The traffic was sporadic—a few scout cars, a tanker truck with two armored cars as escort, a small troop convoy, an occasional motorcyclist. As the time passed, Gideon's impatience grew. He was about to order an attack on the next vehicle of any type that passed by when In'Hout called his attention to a faint rumbling to the east.

"That's it," Brusilov said. "A tank."

"How are we going to stop it?" In'Hout asked.

"I've been thinking," Brusilov replied. "We'll use that wreck fifty meters down the road."

Gideon turned. In the darkness he could barely see the outlines of a German armored car that appeared to have been strafed.

"I think I know what you've got in mind," Gideon said to Brusilov. "Let's be quick."

The three Phoenix members sprinted from their cover to the wrecked vehicle. Brusilov dropped to the ground and opened the drain cock under the engine block. Motor oil flowed out in a thin stream onto the gravelly sand. Brusilov rolled out of the way, then broke open a few 9mm cartridges, trailing a line of powder away from the car.

The tank was closer now, just beyond the bend. Gideon and In'Hout sprawled on the ground in front of the disabled vehicle. Brusilov quickly lit a match. The powder trail ignited, followed by the pool of oil. Thick black smoke clouded the sky. As Brusilov picked up his weapon and darted across the road, the grease on the engine block caught fire, and orange-black flames rose into the night.

Gideon could hear shouts in German over the noise of the approaching Panzer. The tank stopped about ten meters from the burning vehicle. A moment later, a spotlight went on, the beam playing on the armored car, then moving toward Gideon. The Phoenix commander concentrated on remaining motionless. The beam moved off, sweeping the surrounding ground, playing back and forth from east to west. Finally, it swung back to Gideon.

The tank commander remained perched on the turret, still pondering the scene before him. Brusilov, quiet as a cat, had crept to the base of the Panzer. Just as the German officer lowered his head to bark an order, the Russian grabbed the frame of the tank's water-jug holder and swung himself up onto the rear deck. In a quick fluid motion, he seized the chin of the tank commander with his left hand and bent the man's head back, and with his right hand slit his throat. The German's cry became a hideous gurgling as blood gushed down into the tank below.

As soon as Gideon heard the muffled cry, he leaped to his feet, picked up the MP40 that had been concealed beneath him, and dashed for the tank. The 7.92mm machine gun began to sweep toward him, but before it could open fire, Gideon leaped onto the front deck and jammed the muzzle of his weapon into the vision slit. He pulled the trigger, letting loose a sustained burst of 9mm bullets that ricocheted inside the lower compartment. Brusilov let loose a moment later, firing through the turret hatch.

A moment later, it was over. Brusilov set his weapon down, lifted the body of the tank commander, rolled it off the tank, then lowered himself into the vehicle. He quickly returned, pale and gagging. "It's a charnel house below."

"We don't have time to clean up," Gideon said. "In'Hout, run back and get the others. Brusilov, you and I will hoist out the bodies. We've got to get moving before another vehicle comes along."

Twenty minutes later, they passed through the first checkpoint without incident. Charvey, at the controls, slowed as they approached the two guards standing by the small blockhouse near the road. The guards simply waved them on, and Gideon ordered Charvey to accelerate.

Gideon breathed a sigh of relief. They were halfway to Sirte now. One more checkpoint to pass, then they could leave the road. Said recommended circling around to penetrate the airfield from the western side, which was less heavily patrolled. He planned to have a three-man team infiltrate the perimeter of the field, while the tank shelled the terminal building from outside.

Eliska pulled herself up next to Gideon and gratefully inhaled a breath of fresh night air.

Gideon turned to her. "So far, so good."

She nodded, but her expression was somber.

He touched her arm. "Is something wrong?"

She looked at him. "Below, when we were waiting to see what the Germans would do, I remembered that submarine we captured in Norway—the way we were cramped together, the fetid air. But Kinelly was there, growling in that thick Irish brogue."

"I know," Gideon said. "I miss him, too."

She sighed. "And on the last mission, it was Ian who died. So many years of war ahead, and already we are so few. Next time it may be Charvey, or In'Hout, or—"

Gideon bent over and kissed her, cutting off her words. Then he pulled back. "We can't talk like this, not now."

Eliska said, "The mission. Then there will be another mission, and one after that. I've made my choice, I don't regret it. But that can't stop me from wishing for better times."

Gideon had no reply. He kissed her gently again. Then she went below, to give another a turn in the fresh air.

Said joined Gideon. The Phoenix commander was about to ask him a question about the terrain around the airbase when out of the corner of his eye, he saw a flash in the distance. Instinctively, he ducked just before he heard the boom and whistle of a shell passing overhead.

"Off the road!" he screamed at Charvey.

The Frenchman gunned the big Maybach engine and pulled back the right steering lever. The tank turned off the road, then slid left as the treads lost traction in the soft sand.

Gideon saw a sequence of flashes before him. "Four tanks ahead," he shouted. "Brusilov, take the turret cannon. In'Hout and Eliska, get on the machine guns. Charvey, get us the hell out of here!"

The tank was sinking into a hole. Charvey slipped the clutch, slammed the tank into reverse, and accelerated backward. He braked hard, found forward gear again, and revved the engine. The front drive wheels groaned, and the sixteen small road wheels at the bottom of the tracks squealed.

But the tank careened out of the hole and lurched forward just as two shells detonated behind it.

As the tank lumbered over the sand, Brusilov cranked the turret toward the pursuing Panzers. He saw the flash as another shell was launched, then hurriedly dialed his cannon to sight in on the target. He pulled the lanyard just before an enemy shell detonated in front of them. Their tank banged through the crater. When the dust cleared, Gideon saw flames spouting from one Panzer, indicating a direct hit.

But the other tank wasn't fatally crippled. Its cannon fired another shell that whistled overhead. In'Hout swiveled his machine gun and fired long bursts of 7.92mm bullets. Suddenly, there was an explosion and bright-orange flames boiled into the sky.

"What happened?" Said asked Gideon as they stared from the turret.

"Brusilov's shell must have torn a hole in the armor. In'Hout's shots went through the hole to the fuel tank. Now, all we have to do is . . ."

Gidcon's words were drowned by an explosion that showered the tank with sand. "Thirty degrees right!" Gideon shouted.

Charvey obeyed, cutting the tank hard.

Gideon looked into the landscape faintly illuminated by the burning tank. Two of the remaining Panzers had cut off to circle them. The third was coming at them head on.

Working with lightning speed and precision, Brusilov spun the turret around, aimed, and fired. His shell went down the barrel of the German tank, putting it out of commission. His second shell slammed into the turret, which exploded in flame. One German soldier managed to stumble out, but Eliska chopped him down with a short burst from her machine gun.

That left the two tanks. "Head for the road!" Gideon commanded. "Forty-five degrees left."

Charvey zigzagged to throw off the enemy gunners, heading for the hard surface where they could make real speed.

Gideon was grim and tense. Even if they outran the tanks

behind them, the entire German coastal defensive force would be alerted. He expected to hear fighters in the air at any moment. The logical move would be to abandon the tank and flee on foot to the protection of the rocks at the base of the cliffs.

But that would mean abandoning the mission, ensuring that the plans for the XX rocket would get back to Germany. Gideon knew that stopping Ulmer was worth any risk. They'd have to continue and trust to luck for their escape.

A shell exploded ten meters to their right, rocking the tank. Charvey slammed on the brake. "Get a crowbar!" he shouted to Gideon. "The right track is slipping."

Gideon spotted the crowbar and jumped down from the turret as Brusilov swung the gun around. He heard the whistle of another shell and dove under the tank for protection. A second later came the closest explosion of all.

His heart pounding, Gideon jumped out and inspected the right track. The problem was simple. He jammed the crowbar under the front right side of the track and leaned with all his weight. The tread resisted for moment, then shifted back on track.

Gideon had just finished when Brusilov fired. He flinched at the noise, then climbed back in the turret as another German missile rocked the tank. Gideon shouted down to Charvey, who slammed the tank into gear.

The vehicle lurched forward. Brusilov fired another shell, and Gideon felt a jolt of pleasure as he saw the Russian had scored his third direct hit.

He looked ahead once more to see the ridge of the roadbed approaching. The tank curvetted and wheeled over the crest, tossing the Phoenix team about. The treads found hard pavement, and Charvey shifted into cruising gear. The tank accelerated to twenty-five miles per hour, twice its speed in the soft sand.

Gideon kept glancing to the rear, waiting for the flash of the fourth tank's cannon. But he saw nothing. Perhaps the tank commander had stopped to help his wounded comrades.

He spun as he heard a loud boom directly in front of them.

A chill ran through him—the fourth tank had circled around to cut them off, and was now on the road ahead.

Brusilov spun the turret, aimed, and fired. He missed.

"Stop!" Gideon yelled down to Charvey.

"The hell I will," the Frenchman shouted back. "We'd be sitting ducks."

Charvey shifted to maximum speed. The gunner of the tank must have been startled, for the next shell sailed way over their heads. The German commander guessed Charvey's intention, and the Panzer started to back off the road.

But Charvey slammed into it before it could get free. Gideon crashed into the side of the turret as he heard the horrible grinding sound. The other Panzer had been rolled over on its side. Eliska and In'Hout spun their guns and riddled the soldiers trying to scramble from the vehicle.

"Let's get out of here!" Gideon yelled down to Charvey. The tank backed up, clear of the wreckage, and started forward. Gideon heard the engine straining.

"What's wrong?" he yelled to Charvey.

"We lost high gear," the Frenchman replied.

Gideon debated for a moment. "We'd better get off the road. Without speed, we'll be too easy to find."

Charvey obeyed. The tank rolled down the embankment into the soft sand.

Gideon took the opportunity to check for injuries. Eliska had a bruised arm, In'Hout a nasty cut over his eye.

Gideon turned to Said. "How far to Sirte?"

"Maybe five kilometers."

"Good. We'll get as close as we can in the tank, then abandon it. We'll circle the town on foot to get to the airfield."

"Gideon!" Charvey yelled.

"What is it?"

"A barbed-wire fence up ahead."

Gideon saw it now, a six-foot-high barrier, stretching to both sides as far as he could see.

"We have no choice," he said. "Go through it."

The tank chewed up and spit out the wire.

Gideon wondered about the fence. They weren't that close to Sirte. What was it protecting?

The answer suddenly came to Gideon, causing him to break out in a sweat. A minefield. Probably a barrier against British attack.

"Stop!" Gideon yelled to Charvey. "Back up. We've got to—"

But it was too late. The tank violently bucked like a bronco, tilted in midair, then slammed back into the ground, flipping over, as a thunderous explosion cut off Gideon's warning.

CHAPTER FIFTEEN

ONE BY ONE, they crawled from the wreckage through a side turret hatch and collapsed onto the sand. Gideon hurriedly moved from person to person, checking for injuries.

Although everyone was bruised and shaken, no one was badly hurt. The Teller mine had demolished one of the tank's tracks, but it hadn't pierced the armor, nor had the engine caught fire.

Gideon knew that their situation was still desperate. Although they'd destroyed the tanks pursuing them, other German forces must have been alerted. They'd have no chance of reaching the airfield at Sirte and evading capture once the sun rose in little over an hour.

That would have been difficult enough if they were in the tank. But now they were trapped in the middle of a minefield, where a misplaced footstep meant sudden death.

Brusilov had moved to Gideon's side. The Russian had drawn his combat knife, carrying it in his right hand. He pointed the knife toward the darkness of the minefield. "I'll do the honors," he said. "I've cleared many paths in my time."

Gideon said. "No. It's my job as leader to take the risks. I'll—"

"You're both wrong."

Gideon turned to see Eliska beside him. Before he could speak, she continued, "I'm the one who took the minefield training course at Bladesover. The lightest person clears the path. If they're all Teller mines in this field, I could walk out of here safely."

Gideon hesitated for a moment, reluctant to assign the task to anyone but himself. He sighed and matched her tight smile. "You're right," he said. "You know what to do. Just don't rush, no matter how badly you want to get out of here. We'll be about thirty meters behind you."

Eliska nodded, drew her knife, and dropped to all fours.

Gideon watched her probe in the sand with the tip of the knife, inches at a time. When she'd cleared a space of a few feet, she moved up. The rest of the team followed her track in the sand.

The Slovak woman was only five meters from the tank when the tip of her knife touched metal. She probed with her fingers, feeling the lip of the mine. Carefully, she took a bullet from her ammunition belt and placed it in the sand, marking the mine's location. Then she probed cautiously to the left, moving around the obstacle.

It was draining, tedious work. At times, to rest her back and knees, Eliska lay flat on her stomach, reaching out with one hand. Despite the coolness of the night, sweat poured down her brow into her eyes.

Emotionally, the work was excruciating. She wanted to feel the metal of the mines, to know for certain which way not to pass. And she dreaded their touch.

The sense of urgency drove her onward, despite the pain. She had to clear the path before dawn.

Gideon didn't think she'd make it. He led the others on the slow progress down the track Eliska had cleared, staying thirty meters back, while he agonized with her.

The first couple hundred meters had been covered relatively quickly. Then Eliska ran into a forest of smaller, more deadly antipersonnel mines, and she was forced to weave a much slower, tortuous path.

Gideon perceived the faintest traces of light in the eastern skies. At this rate, they'd still have about fifty meters to cross when the sun came up.

Out of desperation, he was considering a new plan. Brusilov

had managed to rescue his Sten, with almost a full clip, from the tank. Raking a path through the minefield with the machine pistol would clear half the distance, Gideon figured.

The rest, he'd take care of. He'd simply pick the shortest distance to the fence marking the border of the minefield and begin walking. He knew the odds were against him. But one death to save six was worth the sacrifice. It was the only way the mission could be saved.

Gideon directed his attention to Eliska. She'd been able to move a little bit faster.

A sound froze his heart. He listened, muscles taut. He felt Brusilov's hand on his arm. "Do you hear? A tank. Or two."

"I hear," Gideon said.

He saw the Russian unsling the Sten.

"No," Gideon ordered. "That's useless against armor. They'll slaughter us."

"Better than being prisoners," Brusilov said fiercely.

"That's my decision," Gideon retorted sharply. "You'll wait for my orders before you . . ."

He stopped as the beam of a powerful searchlight began sweeping the minefield. He held his breath as the circle of light scanned back and forth. Suddenly, it stopped on Eliska's prone form.

Instinctively, he moved forward along the cleared path to join her. As he came into the light, a voice called out in German, "Stay where you are!"

Behind him, Gideon heard the click as a cartridge was chambered in a Sten. "Brusilov, don't fire!" he ordered in English. Then in German, he called out, "We need a map of the minefield."

He heard the sound of arrogant laughter. "You come to us," the German officer commanded in a haughty tone. "We have time to wait."

"Scott," Eliska asked in English. "What do I do?"

"We have no choice. We can't stay here forever—they'll get bored eventually and blast us. At least as Afrika Korps prisoners we'll have a chance to escape. You've got to continue clearing the path."

Eliska moved forward. She found it harder to concentrate as the German tank crews stood at the edge of the minefield in the increasing light, laughing and taunting the trapped Phoenix team. By the time she reached the fence, her face was red with suppressed anger.

The rest of the team followed. An *Oberleutnant* lined them up and ordered them frisked.

The lieutenant strutted up and down in front of them. Then he stopped in front of Gideon. "So you are the saboteurs who attacked the Führer's research bunker."

"Yes," Gideon replied in German, "but attack is the wrong word. You should have said 'destroyed.'"

The German stiffened. "The English, so arrogant. You'll lose that attitude soon."

"We're not all English," Eliska spoke up. "We represent several nationalities who all hate your housepainter and the rest of you Nazi swine."

The lieutenant whirled and slapped her across the face. Brusilov started to move, but Gideon stopped him with a shout.

"So your men obey their leader," the *Oberleutnant* snarled. "Let us see how calm you are while you die."

He turned and barked a command to his men. Thirteen 98k carbines were leveled at the Phoenix team.

Gideon laughed.

The lieutenant's fury increased. "How dare you—"

"How dare you pull off this charade?" Gideon said harshly. "We know the SS wants to interrogate us. If you had us shot you'd be taken in front of a firing squad. You Wehrmacht types are just errand boys."

For a moment, Gideon thought he'd gone too far. Then, getting control of himself, the lieutenant issued an order to his men. "Tie the prisoners, hands to ankles. Take them to the side of the road."

Two soldiers ran for rope. When they returned, the others began tying the hands of the Phoenix team behind their backs. They kicked the feet out from under the captives and rolled them over to bind their wrists and ankles together.

Then the Germans dragged them to the shoulder of the road—two soldiers per prisoner, except for Brusilov, who required three.

Gideon lay with his face in the dust, listening to the jeers of the soldiers. His shoulders, wrists, ankles, and leg muscles were racked with pain, and his mouth was as dry as the desert sands.

The team remained sprawled by the roadside for what seemed like an eternity. Finally a truck came for them, a two-ton Büssing-NAG. They were picked up and thrown on the bed as if they were sacks of grain. The truck lacked a tarpaulin, so the newly risen sun was on their faces, increasing their monumental thirsts.

As Gideon expected, Waffen SS guards armed with automatic weapons stood over them. He was sure they would be taken to SS headquarters. He hoped Ulmer had heard of his capture and would want to interrogate the men who had destroyed his creation. That was their last slim chance to complete their mission.

The ride into Sirte was less than two miles. From the bed of the truck, Gideon soon saw the tops of houses. The truck came to a halt and the Waffen SS guards cut their feet free, ordering the prisoners out of the truck and across the courtyard of a luxurious villa that seemed incongruous in the desolation of the desert town.

The cellar of the villa was reminiscent of other SS dungeons, a series of dark cells fitted with massive steel doors. Stumbling, barely able to walk after having been bound for nearly an hour, the Phoenix members were pushed by twos into cells. Their hands were still tied behind their backs and they were given no water, despite their dehydration. Complaints fell on deaf ears.

Gideon and Said were in the same cell. For hours they lay in virtual silence, trying to regain some of their strength. Finally, the small observation window in the door opened. The light was startling after the blackness. Then the door itself opened, and two guards stood with buckets of water. They doused Gideon, but not Said. Both men tried to catch the dripping water with their tongues. Another guard appeared with a set of clothing. He bent down and cut the cord binding Gideon's wrists.

Tossing the clothing to Gideon, he ordered in German, "Put these on." He turned and closed the door behind him.

Gideon changed into the clothes, then waited. Minutes became an hour. Finally, the door opened and the same three guards ordered Gideon to walk ahead of them down the corridor and up a flight of stairs. At the top, he passed through a guardroom, then was pushed inside an office.

He came face to face with Semmeln Ulmer, who sat behind a desk. Opposite him, slightly to one side, sat Tibor Horvath, who had also been doused with water and given fresh clothing.

Ulmer extended his hand toward a second chair. "Sit down," he said in German.

Gideon sat and scanned the room—one barred window, one door with a room full of guards outside. Not very promising.

As if reading his mind, Ulmer held up a Walther P38. "I wouldn't suggest trying anything. The guards outside will respond instantly to any shout."

Ulmer cleared his throat and continued. "As I was telling our mutual friend Herr Horvath, I've asked permission from the Waffen SS to talk with you both before they begin applying their sophisticated interrogation techniques." He flashed a cold smile. "It's time I knew your real identity."

Gideon looked him steadily in the eye. "My name is Scott Gideon. I'm an American."

Ulmer nodded his wide chiseled face and rubbed his high brow. "An American. I have always thought Americans resourceful. You have confirmed my opinion. You performed remarkably well in your impersonation and in your attack on our facility. You destroyed years of hard labor. We were so close to success. And now, thanks to you, nothing. Only this." He tapped his head.

Gideon merely raised his eyebrows in reply.

Ulmer nodded agreeably. "Yes. You can be sure the enemies of Germany have not heard the last of the XX rocket. I shall have another facility, the Führer has already informed me." He stood up and paced behind the desk, Walther in hand. "Before I roll up my sleeves and begin again, I want to satisfy my curiosity about the *Betonunterstand* affair. How did you find out about the facility?"

"The convoys and test flights gave it away. Did you really expect to keep a project of that scope secret forever?"

"No, just long enough to finish. Who first reported the activity?"

Gideon didn't want to implicate the Bedouins. "British air reconnaissance."

"And who organized and financed your mission?"

Nor did Gideon want the Germans to become aware of Philaix and his extensive endeavors. "The British."

"But why an international team?"

"This was a special operation, requiring special skills. The regular British army was too busy on the northern front to field a team at the moment. Instead, they hired professional mercenaries," Gideon lied.

"Ah, mercenaries. You did it for the money. My project destroyed because of greed." Ulmer shook his head forlornly.

"Not in my case," Horvath spoke up.

"I shall never make the mistake of calling in foreign scientists again. I should have known that you were a Hungarian first and a scientist second."

"And what about you?" Gideon asked. "Are you a scientist before a German? Why don't you put your work to a good cause—stopping the madman Hitler and his Fascism?"

Ulmer laughed. "You do have an astute mind for a mercenary. What a waste. I sense that you are in this war for principles rather than money. Well, let me tell you about my principles. I am a German and always will be. I don't agree with every decision our Führer has made, but now Hitler is Germany and I will work for him. If I were captured, I would never apply my abilities to anything that might harm Germany."

"But you expected me to betray my country?" Horvath said angrily.

"Hungary belongs to Germany now," Ulmer snapped.

"Their destinies are entwined, can't you see that? You had a great future in the Third Reich as an engineer, but now look at you." He shook his head in contempt. "But enough of this philosophizing. I have more questions." He turned back toward Gideon. "How did the British know to plant you at the *Betonunterstand* as Lichter?"

"They found the plane wreck, put two and two together, and set the plan in motion."

"Where did you learn your chemistry?"

"At the University of Brussels."

"I knew you couldn't have deceived me as you did without some kind of authentic background. And your excellent German?"

"Linguistics study in the United States."

"Well, I must say you are a man of high aptitude. It's too bad we can't find some use for you." He shook his head, feigning sadness. "You'll be tortured and shot as a spy."

"What a pity," Gideon said sarcastically.

"Aha, a man with a sense of humor in the face of death. Very admirable. Just a few more questions to satisfy my curiosity. Herr Horvath has already informed me how you managed to get inside, but, tell me, just what did you use for explosives?"

"Limpet mines packed with plastics and thermite with clockwork fuses."

"Your idea?"

"Yes."

"Ingenious, given the compartmental aspect of our facility. And it was your idea to mix the chemicals together to make a gas that would drive the soldiers away?"

Gideon started elaborating on his actions inside the bunker. He wanted to keep the German physicist distracted right up until he attacked him.

He leaned forward on his seat as he talked, ready to spring. Ulmer was still standing, one hand on the desk, the other holding the Walther. Then he turned the gun hand away slightly. "Guards!" he called out.

Three Waffen SS entered the room. An MP40 was stuck in

Gideon's back. Horvath was pulled off his chair by one of the soldiers. The third blocked Gideon's path to Ulmer.

"Enjoy the fruits of your labor," Ulmer said. "I fear we will not see one another again." He looked at an SS trooper. "Take them away."

On the way to his cell, Gideon silently cursed himself for not acting sooner. He looked for opportunities, one last desperate move, but he was guarded so closely he could do nothing.

Angry and restless, he paced about in the darkness as Said slept. It must be night now, he knew. Ulmer was probably on his way to the airport and would be landing in Germany tomorrow morning, about the same time he would be undergoing his brutal interrogation at the hands of the SS.

That chilling thought lingered with Gideon as he continued to walk. He heard activity outside the door—they were coming for him tonight. The lock turned and the door creaked open. In the light from the hall, he saw two shapes, one in front of the other. Instinctively, he retreated into the shadows.

To his amazement, the second man raised his arm and smashed a gun barrel onto the first man's neck. The man somehow stayed on his feet, and the other man struck him again, this time sending him to the floor.

Gideon was about to charge when a voice said, "Gideon, it's me."

"Masucci! How did you—"

"There's no time," the Italian interrupted. "Grab that German's weapon and get into his uniform. We've got to free the others and get out of here."

"Right." Said helped him pull the clothes off the unconscious guard. As they worked, Masucci quickly told them his story. The Italian had managed to escape on a camel from the German patrol as they destroyed the Phoenix camp. His experience with the Tuareg had served him well during the long desert trip northward to Sirte.

Once there, he'd gone directly to the Italian army. The local commander was suspicious at first of Masucci's explanation that he'd been beaten and left in the desert by a group of rowdy off-duty Germans. But doubt gave way to insatiable curiosity when Masucci revealed that he had seen the mysterious German facility in the Great Sand Sea, kept secret from Nazi allies.

Shortly afterward had come word of the Phoenix team's exploits and subsequent capture. Masucci had little trouble convincing the Italian colonel that he could learn from the team's captors more details about the sabotage attack. The curious colonel, on the pretext that Masucci could identify saboteurs who had attacked an Italian facility, had arranged for Masucci to visit the SS headquarters.

When Gideon was ready, he and Masucci headed down the dimly lit hall toward the desk. The Italian stood in front to shield Gideon's face.

Masucci reached the stairwell first, paused at the bottom, then asked the two guards at the table a question in Italian. Irritated, they told him to speak German.

At that instant, Gideon rushed them. He slashed one across the face with the barrel of the machine pistol and fell onto the other, knocking his chair backward. While Masucci finished off the first guard with a heavy blow to the skull with the butt of his Glisenti pistol, Gideon pressed the MP40 into the throat of the other. The German's call for help turned to a gurgling noise as Gideon forced the life from him.

He tossed Masucci the keys. "Free the others. I'll get weapons."

Two minutes later they were all gathered at the bottom of the stairs, ready for an attack on the first floor. Gideon had one MP40, Brusilov and In'Hout the others. Eliska, Charvey, and Said each carried two grenades. Masucci had his pistol. Only Horvath was unarmed.

"Masucci and I will go first. We'll see how far we can get. The front door is to the left. There are a lot of guards in the room to the right. Be ready to back us up with those grenades."

Gideon started up the stairs, followed by the Italian and then the others. At the top, he opened the door a crack. Hearing German laughter, he waved Masucci onward. They stepped into the hallway. To the right it opened into the room through which Gideon had walked on his way to his meeting with Ulmer.

"*Kommen Sie mal her!*" someone called out as they walked left toward the front door.

Gideon whirled and opened fire, raking the room behind him. Charvey jumped out of the cellar door and tossed two grenades in the direction Gideon was shooting. Gideon and Masucci flattened against the far wall next to the front door. The explosions sounded in close succession.

"Watch the front door!" Gideon yelled, then fired again, killing the two Germans who had survived the grenades.

Brusilov and In'Hout stepped out of the stairwell, ready with their automatics. A moment later, a group of four soldiers opened the door and rushed in, only to be met by a wall of bullets. Gideon kicked a limp body out of the way and slammed the door shut again.

Another group of Waffen SS charged from the other end of the hall. Eliska threw a stick grenade underhanded and they fell like bowling pins as the grenade detonated. One bloodied soldier tried to lift himself to shoot, but Masucci fired two quick shots with his Glisenti, obliterating the man's face.

"How many outside?" Gideon asked the Italian.

"Twelve, when I came in," he answered quickly.

"Eight left then. Grenades?"

"I have both of mine," Said answered.

"And I have one," Eliska added.

"In'Hout and Said, see if you can find the way to the roof. Cover us from up there. In exactly three minutes we're coming out. Go!"

The two ran off and the rest of the team waited near the door, ready for a sudden onslaught of Germans.

None came, and an eerie silence descended on them. Gideon watched the second hand of his watch. "Fifteen seconds," he said quietly. "Ready, here we go."

Gideon opened the door with the barrel of his gun, then jumped back as automatic fire riddled the doorway. There was one explosion outside, then another—Said's two grenades. Gunfire resounded from the rooftop—In'Hout's MP40.

Gideon rushed through the door, firing blindly. There was one concentration of enemy fire to the left. Gideon hit the ground, rolling and shooting. Eliska threw her grenade toward the German weapons and dove to the ground next to Gideon.

"Grenade!" Brusilov yelled, mowing down the German who threw it.

The grenade tumbled toward Horvath, who kicked reflexively at it, meeting the grenade squarely with the side of his foot. It bounced away about twenty feet and detonated. The force of the blast knocked Horvath down, a piece of shrapnel ripping into the flesh of his thigh. The scientist pressed himself to the ground and shouted, "I'm all right!"

Again, there was silence, except for the sound of a siren blaring in the night.

"Come on," Gideon yelled to In'Hout and Said. "Move it!"

The heads of the two men disappeared from the roof. The others waited while they raced back down and out the front door. Eliska, Charvey, and Horvath rushed around the littered courtyard, collecting weapons and grenades from the dead Germans.

They were ready to go, and none too soon. The whining engines of German vehicles could be plainly heard on the next street, heading toward them.

"Where's the airfield?" Gideon yelled to Masucci. "We have a job to finish."

CHAPTER SIXTEEN

THEY CROSSED THE yard bordering the SS headquarters, climbed a stone wall, skirted another house, and found themselves on a road. They ducked into the shadows as a group of Italian soldiers ran by.

"Too many soldiers. We'll never make it across town in time," Gideon said, an edge of desperation in his voice. Time was running out. "We've got to get to the airfield fast."

"Look!" Charvey exclaimed.

An Opel Blitz troop carrier had just wheeled around a far corner and was hurtling toward them.

"Take it!" Gideon ordered.

"I've got the driver!" Brusilov shouted, snapping off the safety of his machine pistol. "Someone put a grenade in the rear."

"Got it!" In'Hout answered.

They darted off toward a pile of broken concrete slabs at the side of the road.

As they reached the protection of the concrete, an armored car squealed around the far corner, following the troop carrier.

"Shit," Gideon swore. "Stay low, we're moving." Instantly he led the rest of the team along the front of the house. If the Germans saw them in the shadows, the Spandau machine gun on the armored car would chew them to pieces.

"Spread out," Gideon warned. "Lob your grenades under the armored car as it passes."

Meanwhile, the Opel troop carrier drew even with the concrete slabs. In'Hout ran out first, a grenade in his right hand. Two rows of German faces, lined up on both sides of the truck's bed, turned in surprise at the sight of him. He fused the grenade, flipped it at them, then leaped to the opposite side of the road as the explosion rocked the night. The truck careened off the road and stalled, spilling dead soldiers from the rear.

Brusilov ran toward the truck and triggered a quick burst at a soldier who jumped out of the cab. The armored car was barreling down on him, and, in one lightning-quick move, the big Russian saved his life by diving under the stalled troop carrier. From that vantage point he raked the legs of three soldiers trying to escape from the truck. They crumpled to the ground and he finished them off with two quick bursts.

The gunner on the armored car saw In'Hout and swiveled the Spandau toward him. Realizing bullets couldn't penetrate the steel plating protecting the gun, In'Hout sprinted for cover around the front of the Opel Blitz. The driver's side door swung open as he approached, the driver half in, half out, with a Luger in his hand.

In'Hout crashed into the door, slamming the German's head against the front cab post. The driver slumped, unconscious, as In'Hout found safety behind the Opel.

The armored car's gunner hadn't opened fire, unsure whether German soldiers were still alive in the troop carrier. The Dutchman rolled under the cab to join Brusilov.

At that moment, Gideon hurled the first grenade under the armored car. It exploded exactly below the middle of the vehicle. The concussion lifted the car into the air. But when it landed, it kept moving.

Said's and Eliska's grenades exploded short of their target, and suddenly the awesome Spandau machine gun shrieked out a stream of bullets. Charvey stood amid the fusillade and threw the last grenade. His aim was perfect and the armored car careened off the road, just missing the Opel Blitz, then crashed onto its side, flames licking at the undercarriage.

Brusilov and In'Hout rolled out from under the troop carrier and raced toward the armored car. Jamming the barrels of their automatics into the vision slits, they emptied magazines inside.

"Charvey, start the truck!" Gideon bellowed as he raced toward them. "Masucci, get in the cab with him. Everyone else push, then get in the rear."

Charvey pumped the pedal and turned the key. The engine fired and Charvey shouted in triumph. He found first gear. Slowly, so as not to dig the wheels in any deeper, he eased out the clutch. Despite his caution, the wheels spun wildly in the heavy sand.

"Rock her!" Gideon ordered.

Charvey slammed the gears back and forth between first and reverse while the others rocked in rhythm.

On the fifth forward push, the truck kept moving up onto the road. Gideon jumped in front with Charvey and Masucci.

"The quickest way to the airfield?" Gideon questioned Masucci.

"Take the first left."

Charvey turned.

In the back, the others widened the shrapnel holes in the canvas sides of the troop carrier to use as observation and gun ports.

Masucci directed another left. They were on a straight stretch past a long row of houses. Charvey accelerated.

"Slow down!" Gideon suddenly ordered. "Something's ahead."

"Merde," Charvey muttered. "A roadblock. Italian trucks."

"Is there any way around it?" Gideon asked Masucci.

"No. All turnoffs lead to the Mediterranean, except the one to the airport. And we can't risk the sand."

"Then crash it," Gideon ordered Charvey over the roar of the engine. "Ease up as if you're going to stop, then gun it hard. Any grenades up here?"

"No," Masucci answered quickly. "We'll have to use our machine pistols."

"You can fire across in front of me," Charvey said fiercely to the Italian. "Just don't get carried away."

Masucci nodded, then slammed a magazine into his rifle. Charvey downshifted from second to first.

Soldiers from a truck stepped into the roadway to check the German troop carrier. Charvey shifted into neutral, letting the truck glide. Then with one quick flip of his wrist, he rammed the gearshift into second and stomped on the accelerator.

The Italian soldiers scrambled frantically out of the truck's path. Gideon and Masucci opened fire, killing two men and pinning the others behind their trucks.

Charvey rammed a car, knocking it aside. Inside the car, a man let loose with a Beretta submachine gun, stitching bullets across the truck's windshield just above Charvey's head. Brusilov retaliated instantly, blasting away half the enemy's face.

A German cocked his arm to throw a grenade, but Eliska and In'Hout shot him in the midsection. He jackknifed backward like a puppet on a string before hitting the ground. His grenade went off with a roar.

Suddenly they found themselves through the roadblock, racing down a straight, narrow street.

"That was a temporary roadblock," Masucci shouted as they pulled away. "There's a permanent German checkpoint on the road to the airfield."

"Soft sand all around it?" Gideon asked.

"Right."

Charvey looked through the rearview mirror. "There's traffic behind us."

"An Italian truck?" Gideon asked, twisting around to look out the shattered side window.

"Can't tell. Whatever it is, it's gaining."

"How far to the turnoff?" Gideon asked again.

"Two miles," Masucci replied.

Charvey shook his head. "They'll catch us by then." He glanced back in the mirror. "Wait, the headlights are separating. Motorcycles."

"Jesus!" Gideon growled, "they're probably BMW R75s with machine guns mounted on the sidecars."

The motorcycles continued to gain on them. Gideon's guess

about the motorcycles' weapons proved correct when two MG34s simultaneously opened fire at the truck. Brusilov, In'Hout, Charvey, and Eliska immediately answered back, but the machine pistols didn't have the range of the sidecar-mounted light machine guns.

Charvey twisted the truck violently back and forth across the road, but the fast-approaching motorcycles continued to find the truck with their deadly machine guns.

"Slam on the brakes," Gideon shouted, "and spin us around. My side."

Charvey hit the pedal and jerked the wheel to the right. Shrieking in protest, the back wheels locked and began to skid. The truck turned ninety degrees and screeched to a halt. Phoenix guns sent forth a wall of lead down the road.

The front motorcycle driver couldn't brake in time, and crashed his machine into the side of the truck, splintering it apart as though made of balsa wood.

The second BMW careened past the truck's rear, the driver's quick reaction momentarily saving his life. Charvey and Eliska found his gas tank with a massive, coordinated burst of machine-pistol fire. The BMW 75 exploded and veered wildly to the right, now only a hurtling ball of fire. It hit an embankment at full speed, and flew into the air for the shortest of flights before slamming into an ancient stone cistern and disintegrating.

Charvey wheeled the truck back around and accelerated down the empty road.

Gideon's mind raced with the speeding truck, fearful of the passing minutes. The future of German rocketry would be determined in the coming moments, depending on whether or not Ulmer's plane had taken off.

They made the final turn toward the airport. A half mile to go. They strained to discern shapes in the shadowy, silvery night, knowing a German checkpoint would soon appear.

Then it was ahead of them. Two small stone blockhouses stood on opposite sides of the road with a gate running between them. Another Opel Blitz and an armored car faced one another across the road behind the gate.

"Run it?" Charvey asked grimly.

"No, slow down," Gideon told him. "We'll never make it by that armored car."

"Then we must ram it with the truck. I can jump off at the last second."

"Our only choice," Gideon agreed.

Charvey slowed the truck as Gideon shouted toward those in the back. "Jump out now. When you hear the explosion, go for the other truck." Gideon moved aside to let Masucci climb down. "Charvey and I will join you afterward." Masucci nodded quickly, then jumped.

"You're coming?" Charvey asked, gunning the engine.

Gideon flashed a tight grin. "If I can blow our gas tank, the explosion will take out one of the blockhouses along with the armored car."

Gideon grabbed an oily rag and a distress flare from the floor of the cab, opened the passenger door, and stepped out onto the running board. Charvey had reached third gear and was holding the truck steady at twenty-five kilometers per hour. Bracing himself with his right hand, Gideon crouched down and unscrewed the fuel cap. He jammed the rag into the full gasoline tank, twisting it into a makeshift fuse.

"Hurry!" Charvey shouted.

Ahead, the Germans at the checkpoint were scrambling out of the truck's path.

"Ready?" Gideon yelled.

Charvey swung open his door in response. Gideon struck a match, lighting the flare. "Go!" he shouted, thrusting the burning flare into the oil-soaked rag as Charvey jumped free.

The intense heat from the flare ignited the rag, and Gideon jumped. The Opel Blitz, now a rolling bomb, plowed square into the side of the armored car and exploded in a huge, brilliant flash. The rear of the truck swung around to the left and slammed into the front of the blockhouse, shooting flames inside.

Momentarily stunned by his fall, Gideon struggled to his feet. He saw Charvey running for the truck on the other side of the road. Ahead, the rest of the Phoenix team were blasting the soldiers who were trying to exit the second blockhouse.

Charvey jumped into the new truck and cranked the engine to life. When the others heard the rumble they piled in the rear. Gideon raced to join them as Eliska, In'Hout, and Brusilov provided covering fire.

Charvey jammed the truck into first gear. Gideon grabbed the door handle and jumped onto the running board, then yanked open the door and slid onto the seat. Charvey gunned the engine to maximum speed, and they raced away from the fiery hell they had created.

Gideon, panting, exhaled a sigh of relief. "There should be nothing left now between us and the airfield."

"Tank ahead!" Charvey screamed back at him.

Gideon jerked his head up. "That's not a tank. It's a Hummel!"

The big self-propelled gun opened up with a burst of flame from the gaping muzzle. A shell screamed five yards over the truck and exploded thunderously behind them.

"Get off the road," Gideon yelled.

"What about the sand?" Charvey shouted back.

"No choice!"

Charvey swung the truck sharply off the road to the left. A fraction of a second later a shell screamed by on their right. The truck plowed through the soft sand, momentum carrying it. The Hummel rolled backward on its tracks, following the truck with its barrel.

"Hard right!" Gideon screamed, watching the Hummel's movement.

Charvey swerved to the right at the last possible moment, as a perfectly placed shell exploded in their former path.

The Opel's rear wheels hit deeper sand and spun out. Charvey instantly eased up on the gas and downshifted to hold his forward motion. The truck labored for an agonizing moment, then pulled ahead, just fast enough to avoid a howitzer volley, erupting ten yards to its rear.

"Back on the road. Head directly for the Hummel," Gideon ordered.

The truck bumped over the rough shoulder, found pavement, and picked up speed toward the self-propelled gun as the huge cannon swung toward them. One hit and the truck would be demolished.

"Right," Gideon yelled.

Charvey jerked the wheel at the exact instant the Hummel fired. The shell screamed by them. The truck roared past the Hummel and Phoenix guns raked its rectangular superstructure, riddling the crew of five with hot lead.

"Got them," Gideon shouted triumphantly. "Now the airfield."

Gideon knew all their valiant efforts would be wasted if they failed to stop Ulmer's departure. This was it. There would be no more chances.

In the distance they could make out a tower, a chain-link fence, hangars, runways, and two rows of planes facing each other—Junkers Ju 86s, 87s, and 88s. At the end of the road leading up to the airfield was a gate and a guardhouse. Fifteen sentries were lined up across the road in front of the entrance, ready with their machine pistols.

"Straight ahead?" Charvey asked, hesitating for the first time.

"Crash the gate. We're gonna cripple those planes."

Charvey clenched his teeth and gunned the engine to its red-line maximum. German bullets slammed into the front of the racing truck, perforating metal and shattering glass.

"Duck!" Gideon yelled suddenly. The Frenchman, head below the dash, held the wheel at the bottom, keeping what he prayed was a straight course. Crouched in the back, the others held the barrels of their MP40s over the sides of the truck bed, fingers pressed on triggers, blindly emptying magazine after magazine at the enemy.

The truck roared through a hail of gunfire toward the remaining Nazis. At the last moment, the soldiers leaped out of the speeding truck's path. A split second later it crashed through the gate.

Covered with glass and wood fragments, Charvey and Gideon rose in their seats. The front of the truck was smashed and riddled with bullet holes, but the engine, though spewing steam, kept running.

Air-raid klaxons shrieked as the Phoenix team finally rolled into the airfield.

"Drive right between the planes," Gideon directed. "We'll make sure Ulmer can't use any of them."

Charvey steered the truck down the middle of the two rows of parked bombers. Gideon opened fire at a Stuka, pouring lead into the engine cowling. A moment later, the dive bomber burst into flames, belching a thick cloud of black smoke.

As Gideon reloaded, the rest of the team fired from the truck bed. In a matter of minutes, the airfield was a raging, wild inferno, bombs and ammunition going off in a chain reaction, crippling planes not directly hit by machine-pistol fire.

As the truck neared the end of the row, the engine began to fail. Charvey brought the Opel to a stop in a cloud of smoke and steam.

Gideon hit the gravel first. Ahead, near a hangar, was a fuel truck. Gideon opened fire, raking the vehicle with two full clips. A strong smell of gasoline assaulted him, followed by a violent explosion which nearly knocked him off his feet. A wall of jagged flame roared into the night, the heat scorching Gideon's face.

He turned away from the glare to see the rest of the team behind him. "Come on!" he shouted. "Find Ulmer!"

Phoenix sprinted across the blazing airstrip. As they neared the last in a line of four hangars, the door swung open. Two firetrucks, warning horns blaring, bore down on them. With no time to run for cover, they held their positions and opened fire, aiming for the windshields. Brusilov killed one driver with a short burst, causing the truck to swerve left into the other vehicle. The second driver lost control, and both firetrucks careened into a burning plane. A tremendous explosion rained hot debris on the black runway.

Gideon led the team around the side of the hangar away from the fires.

"What now?" Brusilov asked.

Gideon looked at the Russian. Like the rest, he was coughing from the smoke, his face covered with grease, soot, and sweat.

A thought suddenly struck Gideon—they had no way out. They'd just destroyed all of the airplanes which might have carried them to freedom. Using the safe house in Sirte was out of the question. And they'd never make it back to the coastal road, which would be swarming with Nazis and Italians.

Gideon's mind lingered on the dilemma for a moment. Then he pulled himself together. If they were going to die, Ulmer was going to die with them. But they had to find him first.

Someone yelled, "Gideon! Look!"

He sprinted down the length of the hangar toward In'Hout, who was pointing into the darkness.

Another runway stretched diagonally away from them toward the northwest. At the far end, Gideon saw the running lights of a large airplane, possibly a Junkers Ju 52 like the ones Phoenix had destroyed.

"Ulmer must be on that plane!" Gideon exclaimed.

"No," In'Hout replied, grabbing Gideon's arm. "Over there."

Gideon turned to his left. A staff car, siren whining, was speeding along the chain-link fence on the south side of the airfield to avoid the attack. As Gideon watched, the car turned north toward the plane.

"That's got to be Ulmer," Gideon said. "We must get to that plane."

"We'll never make it across open ground," Brusilov said. A squad of twenty German soldiers were running toward them from the farthest of the four hangars.

Gideon had formed a plan. "In'Hout, you and I will go for the plane. The rest of you lay down as much covering fire as you can. Now!"

Gideon and In'Hout ran down the runway toward the waiting airplane. Behind them, Brusilov and the others opened fire. If the rest of Phoenix could keep the Germans occupied, he and In'Hout had a chance; the staff car was still several hundred meters from the plane.

A round of bullets kicked up in front of Gideon. He veered sharply left, off the runway into the soft sand. In'Hout moved with him, keeping a distance of ten yards so one burst couldn't take them both out. More fire passed over their heads, and Gideon, lungs and legs aching with exertion, bent lower.

From behind them, he heard a savage sustained burst of fire, followed by piercing screams. The firing stopped abruptly. A jolt of satisfaction went through Gideon—Brusilov and the others had done their job.

Gideon turned right, back to the hard surface of the runway. The plane, a Junkers, was only a hundred meters away.

Suddenly, the staff car came into view. It screeched to a halt and a man jumped out and darted for the plane. A crew member helped him up onto one of the wings and through the door.

In'Hout, on the run, opened fire on the two men who had jumped out of the staff car. His first bullets fell short, ricocheting off the runway, but he kept firing to cover Gideon, who headed directly for the plane. In'Hout caught the two Germans as they knelt to fire at the Phoenix leader. They tumbled, dead, to the tarmac.

The engines of the Junkers revved up to takeoff speed. The pilot released the brake and the plane shot forward. Gideon was momentarily caught flat-footed; then he sprinted toward the aircraft.

The success of the mission depended now on Gideon's timing. In seconds, the plane would be acceleratng too fast. With a final burst of speed, Gideon reached the Junkers' wing. Fighting the engine backwash, he jumped onto the wing and held tightly. He looked up to see the pilot's head swing toward him, an expression of almost comical astonishment adorning his face. The Phoenix leader, pressed against the wing, moved up its surface, the roaring wind pushing powerfully at him.

The Junkers' speed picked up, the huge engines screaming into the night. Gideon knew he had only moments left before the force of the wind would yank him off the wing like a paper doll. Teeth clenched, Gideon grasped for a handhold on the fuselage and struggled to his knees.

He saw the Nazi pilot hunched over his stick, pulling back in preparation for liftoff. It was now or never. Gideon stood up in the terrific wind, draping his body against the cockpit for support. The pilot turned toward him, horror etched across his Aryan features as Gideon pressed the muzzle of the MP40 against the cockpit glass. He squeezed the trigger and bullets shattered the glass, ripping into the pilot's neck and killing him instantly.

The engines' roar continued as the copilot held the stick full back. Gideon fired again and the copilot fell against the other side of the cockpit. The engines died abruptly and the speeding Junkers immediately began to slow.

At full sprint, In'Hout rapidly closed in on the slowing plane.

"Watch the tail gunner!" Gideon screamed at him.

A machine gun chattered and Gideon watched helplessly as bullets danced around the Dutchman's feet. Still he kept coming, MP40 unslung. In'Hout pressed off a burst and there was the sound of glass shattering. He fired again. The tail gunner tumbled from the bottom of the plane and landed on the runway, dead.

The plane slowed and rolled to a stop, half off and half on the runway. Gideon jumped down to meet In'Hout.

They spotted the rest of Phoenix running toward them, their angle of approach allowing for the plane's forward motion. There were no Germans in pursuit.

The plane's engines died and the wing flaps lowered automatically. "We've got to get in," Gideon said. "But be careful—there's no way of knowing how many are left inside."

He and In'Hout opened fire at a door in the fuselage. Their bullets pinged back at them. The door held fast.

"If I break more glass, I think I can fit through the cockpit window," In'Hout suggested.

"I'll boost you," Gideon said.

They jumped up on the wing. In'Hout smashed at the already broken glass with the handle of his MP40. When he'd cleared the largest shards, Gideon gave him a boost. He managed to wriggle through, cutting himself in several places.

The others ran up.

"Look!" Eliska warned.

A tank was rounding the farthest hangar at the end of the runway.

Still on the wing, Gideon looked down at Charvey. Until his death during the last Phoenix mission in Norway, Ian Wladyslaw had been the Phoenix pilot. Since then, the Frenchman had been undergoing intensive training to take his place. But he hadn't been tested in combat.

"Charvey, think you can fly this thing?" Gideon asked.

"I can try," Charvey said grimly as he climbed up on the wing.

Suddenly, a burst of automatic fire came from inside the Ju 52. Gideon held his breath. If Ulmer or his escort had gotten the drop on In'Hout, Phoenix was doomed.

The clicking sound of the latch on the wing door was like the sound of music. Gideon breathed a sigh of relief as he saw In'Hout swing the door open. The Phoenix team hurried inside, and Horvath, Said and Masucci then followed as a 75mm shell from the tank's cannon exploded fifty meters from the plane, cratering the runway behind them.

"Hurry!" Gideon shouted to Charvey. "Get her started up. Brusilov, go forward with him. Eliska, you look for parachutes."

He then turned to In'Hout. "Where's Ulmer?"

"He's got to be in the cargo bay," the Dutchman replied. "I killed his two guards."

The Junkers' engine sputtered to life. Gideon heard Charvey building RPMs amid the explosion of another cannon shell, this one closer.

He turned his attention back to In'Hout. "We've got Ulmer trapped. We'll just let him stew in there until—"

A pistol shot rang out in the cargo bay. Then another.

Gideon was puzzled for a moment. Then it struck him. "Ulmer's trying to hit the fuel tank," he shouted to In'Hout. "I've got to take him."

He moved to the cargo door, which had only a latch instead of a lock. His MP40 ready in his right hand, he released the latch with his left and pushed.

Ulmer's arm reached out, grabbed Gideon's neck, and yanked him into the cargo room. The two men fell against the open door, slamming it shut. An instant later, the cold steel of a pistol barrel pressed into Gideon's temple.

The plane was rolling down the runway as Ulmer spat out in German, "Order your men to stop the plane or I'll kill—"

Gideon ducked and, in the same motion, slammed the butt of his MP40 into Ulmer's solar plexus. The German's pistol went off, sending a bullet singing through Gideon's hair. The Phoenix leader smashed Ulmer with his shoulder, sending the scientist crashing into the fuselage.

But Ulmer didn't drop his weapon. He aimed and fired again, blowing a hole in the sheet metal four inches to the left of Gideon's head. Gideon swung and caught Ulmer's pistol with the barrel of his MP40. The pistol fell to the floor. Ulmer launched himself at Gideon, seizing the Phoenix leader's neck in a powerful two-handed grip. Fueled by desperation, adrenaline pumping, the scientist's strength was amazing.

"Die!" the Nazi shrieked. "Die!"

Gideon's air supply was nearly depleted. Dark clouds gathered in his mind as he fumbled for his weapon lying somewhere out of sight on the cargo floor.

Ulmer tightened his grip. Gideon's lungs burned as he inched to his right. Then his fingers wrapped around the barrel of the MP40. He pulled it to him with his last strength and with a final effort, he twisted the weapon and found the trigger.

Bullets spit out. Ulmer's body jerked wildly, then slumped back. Gideon felt blood splash on his hands.

Gideon struggled to his feet. Still shaking, he staggered toward Ulmer. The scientist twitched, then lay still. Gideon knelt to check his pulse. Nothing.

He felt a wave of intense satisfaction. The German XX rocket program was finished.

Another shell exploding on the runway startled Gideon. He

stood and opened the cargo door. Now the team could concentrate on making their escape.

Gideon made his way forward, feeling the transport plane pick up speed. He reached the cockpit as another shell exploded to the rear of the aircraft.

Charvey's face registered complete concentration as he maintained a white-knuckled grip on the yoke. Brusilov was next to him, anxiously monitoring the ground-speed gauge and tachometer.

The tank was now behind them. They'd evaded everything the Germans had thrown at them. But they would be killed if Charvey couldn't get the plane into the air.

The end of the runway was approaching with incredible speed. Charvey took an audible breath, then pulled back on the yoke.

Climb, climb, Gideon's mind screamed. The soft sand was now visible, barely fifty meters ahead. Charvey pulled back harder on the yoke.

The nose of the plane suddenly lifted and the wheels left the ground. The plane climbed slowly, wobbling slightly. Charvey fought with the yoke as the aircraft struggled into the air. Gideon's heart nearly stopped when the nose dropped suddenly. But Charvey applied more power and the Junkers began to climb confidently into the sky.

They'd made it.

Eliska embraced Gideon. A big grin on his face, Charvey called out, "Where the hell are we going? Don't you think the pilot ought to know?"

"Cairo," Gideon said. "I think Philaix owes us a dinner that would put the pharaohs to shame."

**RESISTANCE SERIES #6:
BALKAN BREAKOUT**

Here's the first chapter from
BALKAN BREAKOUT, the sixth action packed
book in the **RESISTANCE** series—about the Phoenix
team's newest mission. . . .

CHAPTER ONE

Flames leaping from one wing, the Zerstörer spiraled downward and plunged into the dark Ionian Sea.

Scott Gideon, observing from the side window of an RAF Anson transport, breathed a long sigh of relief. Close, much too close. The mission to Greece could have been over before it even started because of a freak encounter with a Messerschmitt 110 flying a coincidental night patrol.

But the *Faithful Annie*'s pilot had been good, and so had the air gunner. When the Zerstörer had come at them from behind and above with its nose guns spitting lead, Captain Mackie had made a steep climbing turn to the left, then had flown head-on toward it, making a last-second dip under its belly. A bold move, but it had paid off. Sergeant Brennan, in the dorsal turret, had let loose a series of snap bursts on his belt-fed Browning machine gun that had slammed into the enemy's port engine and windscreen, sending the big gray bird down.

"Stay in the turret, sergeant," Mackie said through his phones to Brennan. "There might be other 110s or a 109 escort around."

Excerpt From BALKAN BREAKOUT

He turned to the wireless operator just behind him. "Corporal Perkins, when the time comes, you help our friends out the door, then kick the supply chutes out after them."

"Yessir, I've got it," Perkins replied in mock seriousness. "Help the supply chutes out the door and boot our friends out after them, righto."

Gideon, on his metal-framed canvas seat in the compartment behind them, heard their words over the hum of the engines and laughed. The corporal hadn't given a straight response yet since Cairo. Captain Mackie didn't seem to mind, and the radioman's enthusiastic sense of humor helped keep the Phoenix team relaxed, despite the strong undercurrent of tension.

"Nice flying," Gideon commented through the hatch.

"RAF—Red-hot Ace Fighters," Perkins joked.

The dark indigo water below suddenly turned to land; the rugged shoreline of central Greece at the western end of the Gulf of Corinth.

"Forty miles to the drop zone," Mackie announced. "Fifteen minutes."

The twin Armstrong Siddeley engines droned on, carrying the *Faithful Annie* closer to Phoenix's destination—the mountainous country of central Greece, called Roumeli by its inhabitants. There, lodged high up in the Agrapha chain, about twenty-five miles west of their drop zone, between the tiny villages of Prousos and Thermos, was the fortress of Massia, the target of this mission.

Gideon knew his obsession with it was just beginning. The ancient stronghold would eventually consume him, body and mind, as it had consumed other attackers centuries before, Athenians trying to rescue their abducted women and children. Already Gideon felt a restlessness that could be exorcised only through action.

There were three-hundred prisoners at Massia. British officers who had been captured when the Wehrmacht tide had swept over Greece the spring before, men desperately needed for the North African campaign. Resistance leaders from all over Eastern Europe, needed to organize the underground fight. And troublesome prisoners of all ranks from other internment camps, men of tenacity and stubbornness who would be valuable to the Allied war.

Excerpt From BALKAN BREAKOUT

Valuable men now. But men how much longer? Massia was more than just an internment camp; it was also an experimental station for the purpose of studying the human will and how best to shatter it.

News of this prison camp had reached the British High Command through the elaborate "Prometheus" underground communications network set up by the resistance since the fall of Greece in April of 1941. Prometheus had reported that native workmen had been forced to turn the ancient fortress of Massia into a high-security prison. A special Waffen SS garrison had surpervised the workmen, then massacred them when the work had been completed. Only one man escaped, making his way to the monastery at Prousos. The Germans had eventually found and killed him, as well as the monks, but not before word had been sent on the long route to Cairo.

The British High Command immediately turned to H. Auguste Philaix and his extraordinary commando team. Phoenix's reputation had soared after their last mission in the Sahara desert, the destruction of a major rocket-testing site. They'd stayed on in Egypt to train in desert warfare with the new British guerrilla force, the Secret Air Service. The British, tied down in Libya and unable to mount any action in Europe, knew that the liberation of Massia was the kind of high-risk mission for which Philaix had founded Phoenix.

For the two weeks after the British had contacted Philaix, the Phoenix team had concentrated on honing their already considerable combat skills, while Philaix made preparations for the mission. The team was fully equipped; a reliable Greek with the contacts needed to accompany them was found and trained; a plane and crew for the flight across the Mediterranean was lined up, as well as a ship to meet and evacuate the prisoners.

But the preparation and planning to date were only the beginning. Phoenix needed more intelligence, help from Greek patriots, if the assault on the fortress was to succeed. Gideon saw the work before the team could attempt their final operation in four stages. Learn the layout and vulnerable points of Massia—an archaeologist in Athens who had worked on the fortress before the war would be their contact. Seek help from the Klephts, the partisan mountain bandits, for the attack on the site and for escort to the coast. Get arms for the evacuees, in case they had to fight. And make arrangements for fishing

Excerpt From BALKAN BREAKOUT

caiques to carry them to the rescue ship. Then the breakout itself. They had a week and a half to carry out the entire mission. It was November 28, 1941, and the British rescue ship would sail off the coast on December 7.

Christ! Gideon thought. What an undertaking.

"Five minutes," Mackie said from the cockpit.

The Phoenix team stood to help one another with their packs, then clipped their parachute catches one by one onto the taut overhead wire. Nearby, in a neat row, were the equipment bundles and containers with folded parachutes on top, ready to be pushed out after them.

If any fighting force of six could pull it off, it was Phoenix, Gideon reflected as Perkins went from person to person, checking the catches. Avrahm Brusilov, Marcel Charvey, and Joel In'Hout, like Gideon, had been with the team from its inception, through five previous missions. Eliska Dobrensky had joined them on their second mission, to Hungary. Gideon, their commander, could depend on them and trust their instincts, undercover or in battle.

Aris Zotos, the new recruit, had experience fighting both Italians and Germans. Before the war he had been a cab driver in Athens. As a soldier he had escaped the closing panzer vise, had hijacked a *Kübelwagen*, and had driven five British soldiers to the southern tip of the Peloponnesus to evacuate. He was what the Greeks called a Brouklis, their bastardization of "Brooklynite," having lived in America for several years during the twenties. Zotos spoke excellent English and could act as an interpreter. He also had connections in the EAM—the Ethniko Apeleftherotiko Metopo, or National Liberation Front, the Greek patriotic movement. And he hated Nazis with a vengeance.

A red light clicked on over the fuselage door.

"Two minutes to go," Perkins told them as he slid open the panel, his tone serious now.

The six commandoes, cold wind whipping their faces, stood in line along the fuselage's metal-ribbed and metal-plated wall, ready to jump, as the plane shuddered to reduced speed. Brusilov bent down one last time to check the bundle that held his latest preferred weapon, a flamethrower. In the cockpit, Mackie, hands working the control stick and throttle levers, moved his eyes from the night outside to his instruments, then

Excerpt From BALKAN BREAKOUT

back outside. In the gun turret, Brennan watched for the sudden swoop of an enemy plane.

Seconds passed. A minute.

The green light clicked on.

"Good luck, mates," Perkins spoke.

"Kalo taxidi," Zotos said. "Happy journey."

Brusilov went first, a huge dark shape launching through the door into the nothingness outside—feet and knees together in a crisp, perfect jump—then Charvey, In'Hout, and Dobrensky, with equal skill.

Zotos stepped forward, tilted a little too far to the left under the load of his big rucksack, and hesitated just before jumping. His left shoulder caught the doorframe and his arm jerked upward in reaction at the same instant he tried to jump. He jerked up and out and hung there, pummeled by the fierce wind. Gideon quickly grabbed his arm and freed him. Zotos catapulted all the way out, his arm scraping the edge of the door. He vanished from sight.

Gideon didn't wait for Perkins's tap, but leaped right out after the Greek. He wanted to stay close to Zotos in case the Greek had problems in the air.

His concern was justified. Just after he felt the jerk of his own chute opening and settled into a comfortable float, he spotted the Greek. Zotos was partly ensnarled in his cords, dangling and swinging at an awkward, dangerous angle. His chute was spilling air and dropping faster than it should.

Damn, Gideon swore. They desperately needed the Greek in order to carry out the mission.

But there was nothing he could do now. Gideon shot a glance back upward to see the supply chutes billowing above him. At least there wasn't a wind tonight to scatter them all over the rugged mountains. They'd be able to rendezvous quickly—if Zotos was alive.

Gideon drifted down through the cold, dark night—fast, but not too fast, thanks to the marvelous properties of nylon, the new synthetic fabric. He watched as the shadowy earth, rocks, and trees rose up at him.

He landed smoothly in a small clearing of ankle-high ground cover, yielding just enough to absorb the blow, even managing to stay upright. Wasting no time, he opened the quick-release

Excerpt From BALKAN BREAKOUT

harness clasp, pulled in on the shrouds, collapsed the parachute, then hid the chute under a nearby rock.

His MP40 cradled in his arms, he jogged southwestward along the drop line to look for the others. Every ten yards or so, he stopped to listen.

Soon he heard the sound he wanted—a plaintive cooing signal—coming from the other side of a stand of pine trees. He answered, then started through the trees.

He came upon a larger clearing. Then he saw Eliska, who had just managed to maneuver over a row of trees. She'd landed too hard, knocking the wind out of herself momentarily. But by the time Gideon had folded and hidden her chute, she was back on her feet.

"You stay put here," he told her. "Keep signaling to draw the others. We'll search for the supplies together, after I find Zotos."

Eliska nodded, and Gideon hurried off. He cut east, where the Greek had been falling. That part of the valley sloped steeply upward to an expanse of bare rock and was a precarious place for a landing—doubly so at the speed Zotos had been descending.

Gideon trudged uphill for about a hundred yards, then stopped to signal. There was no response. He moved on as fast as he could on the treacherous rock surface now underfoot, stopped, and tried again. This time an answer came from even higher on the rock face.

Gideon had to use his hands to climb now. He threaded a gap between two huge boulders, careful not to slip against the jagged surface. Then he saw the chute, reflecting moonlight above, snagged on one of a clump of pine trees that jutted out from a fissure on the rock face. Because of the near-horizontal angle of the tree, it had broken Zotos's fall before he could slam into the granite. He dangled there, bruised and shaken from the violent jerk, but miraculously alive.

"I was ready to release my harness and take a chance on the fall," he called down to Gideon. "I can barely move my arms for lack of circulation."

"Hold on another few minutes," Gideon shouted back.

Strapping his MP40 over his shoulder, Gideon grabbed a handhold overhead, found a cranny for his right foot, and started up the steep face. There were plenty of grooves and ledges on the surface for support, and soon he reached the

Excerpt From BALKAN BREAKOUT

bottom of the fissure. He worked his way up along it to the tree, then straddled the trunk and pulled himself out along the rough bark, scraping his hands and getting them sticky with strong-smelling resin. When halfway out, he extended his arm and grabbed a handful of rope.

"You've got to hold onto the trunk when I pull," Gideon said.

"I will," Zotos gasped.

Gideon, extending himself precariously, grabbed for the Greek's outstretched hand. After several tries, their fingers met. Gideon pulled, his shoulder muscles aching, until Zotos got a grip on a tree limb.

Then Gideon released the Greek's hand and unsnapped the parachute harness. Zotos managed to support his weight until Gideon seized his collar and heaved upward. The Greek got a leg on the trunk and rolled on top.

For a moment, both men were too out of breath to speak. Then Zotos said, *"Efharisto,"* expressing his thanks. Rubbing his shoulders to restore his circulation, he asked, "What about my chute?"

Gideon grimaced. "It'll have to stay exposed, even though it's a calling card. We've got to get moving."

They had crawled to the base of the tree when they heard voices off to the northeast. The others? But Gideon had ordered Eliska to stay put. He and Zotos froze, waiting, straining to hear.

The voices were Italian. A moment later Gideon picked out the shapes in the moonlight—a patrol of six men approaching along the bottom of the hillside. The conversation grew excited for a moment when the Italians caught sight of the snagged chute, then stopped altogether as the patrol began creeping silently and cautiously upward.

Gideon thought hard, weighing the possibilities and consequences. He and the Greek should take out the patrol silently. But there was no way to do that from their exposed, elevated position so near the chute. They'd have to attack first and forget about the noise.

Gideon inched his right hand toward the grenades on his belt, and with his left he unslung his MP40. With his pack on, Zotos was unable to get at his Sten. He pulled his Enfield revolver from his belt.

Gideon waited until the Italians were within twenty meters

Excerpt From BALKAN BREAKOUT

before he stood upright against the rock face and threw the grenade out from the trees toward them. It detonated about five meters above the ground in a blinding flash of light and an enveloping roar.

Agonized screams pierced the night as bodies were flung to the ground. Gideon swung his machine pistol into firing position and triggered sustained bursts at the shapes that still moved.

"Aera!" Zoros shouted the ancient Greek war cry from his seated position and fired down at the closest Italian, catching him in the chest and stomach with his third and fourth shots.

Another Italian fired back—a steady stream of single shots—his bullets chipping rock and splintering wood. Gideon blindly raked the rocks below with a long stream of bullets, then stopped shooting.

The silence seemed overwhelming. Gideon waited a few moments, then started to descend. As he came into view, a slug thudded into the tree two inches from his head. Hurriedly, the Phoenix leader pulled himself back into the cover of the branches. Gideon grabbed a second grenade, pulled the pin, and hurled it down the slope. It exploded in another billowing ball of light.

Then came another pause. Gideon and Zotos waited, listening, looking. This time the silence held. Still, because of the uneven rock shapes below and the dim light, they couldn't be absolutely sure they had killed all six Italians.

They edged slowly downward along the fissure. When they reached the end, Gideon took Zotos's pack to make the rest of the descent easier for him. They couldn't rush this part, groping for support with feet and hands.

Finally, they touched bottom. They heard a moaning—a wounded soldier. Gideon turned toward the prostrate man. Zotos put a hand on his arm. "This is for me to do."

Gideon nodded. They couldn't leave any survivors. The longer Phoenix's arrival went undiscovered, the more distance they could cover from the drop zone to other hills and valleys. And Zotos deserved the opportunity early in the mission to vent some of the fury he felt toward the invaders of his homeland. Later he could learn, as the rest of them had, not to let anger cloud judgment.

Zotos soon returned, wiping and resheathing his knife. "It is done."

Excerpt From BALKAN BREAKOUT

At that instant, Gideon heard a boot scraping on rock. He swung his gun barrel toward the noise. But before he pulled the trigger, he heard the signal. He dropped the barrel of his gun.

Charvey, Sten in hand, came into view. Behind him, also poised and ready for battle, was In'Hout.

"Italians," Gideon explained, gesturing. "A patrol of six. Come on, let's gather up our equipment and get the hell out of this valley. Where's Eliska?"

"Waiting at the landing zone. When we heard the guns and grenades, we came running."

"Any sign of Brusilov?" Gideon asked.

"Not yet," Charvey replied.

They started back to the clearing and broke into grins as they spotted Brusilov. The giant Russian explained that he'd landed on top of a tree, had had a hard time getting down, then had wandered too far to the north before realizing his mistake and circling back.

Gideon gave the order to begin gathering the weapons and supplies the British plane had dropped. The plan had been to hide the weapons in the hills for the time being. Now, because of the Italian patrol, they had to haul them at least out of this valley to a more distant cache.

Strapping on their packs and spreading out, they worked their way northeastward along the valley in the direction the supply chutes had drifted. After about a quarter of a mile, at a point where the valley dipped off through a pass to a lower valley, Eliska spotted a splash of white.

They angled toward this first chute, eager to make the recovery. Then Gideon stopped abruptly, halting the others. Coming the other way, spread out across the width of the sloping pass, was a group of at least two dozen soldiers dressed in mottled camouflage clothing.

Gideon's heart froze. They were the crack Waffen SS troops of the Karstjäger Mountain Division, heavily armed and experienced in waging war in this rugged terrain. And they were sweeping directly toward Phoenix.

JOIN THE RESISTANCE READER'S PANEL

If you're a reader of RESISTANCE, New American Library wants to bring you more of the type of books you enjoy. For this reason we're asking you to join the RESISTANCE Reader's Panel, so we can learn more about your reading tastes.

Please fill out and mail this questionnaire today. Your comments are appreciated.

1. The title of the last paperback book I bought was:
   TITLE: _____ PUBLISHER: _____

2. How many paperback books have you bought for yourself in the last six months?
   ☐ 1 to 3   ☐ 4 to 6   ☐ 7 to 9   ☐ 10 to 20   ☐ 21 or more

3. What other paperback fiction have you read in the past six months? Please list titles: _____
   _____
   _____
   _____

4. My favorite is (one of the above or other): _____

5. My favorite author is: _____

6. I watch television, on average (check one):
   ☐ Over 4 hours a day ☐ 2 to 4 hours a day ☐ 0 to 2 hours a day
   I usually watch television (check one or more):
   ☐ 8 a.m. to 5 p.m.   ☐ 5 p.m. to 11 p.m.   ☐ 11 p.m. to 2 a.m.

7. I read the following numbers of different magazines regularly (check one):
   ☐ More than 6   ☐ 3 to 6 magazines   ☐ 0 to 2 magazines
   My favorite magazines are: _____

For our records, we need this information from all our Reader's Panel Members.

NAME: _____

ADDRESS: _____

CITY: _____ STATE: _____ ZIP CODE: _____

8. (Check one) ☐ Male   ☐ Female

9. Age (check one): ☐ 17 and under   ☐ 18 to 34   ☐ 35 to 49
   ☐ 50 to 64   ☐ 65 and over

10. Education (check one):
    ☐ Now in high school   ☐ Graduated high school
    ☐ Now in college   ☐ Completed some college
    ☐ Graduated college

11. What is your occupation? (check one):
    ☐ Employed full-time   ☐ Employed part-time   ☐ Not employed
    Give your full job title: _____

Thank you. Please mail this today to:
RESISTANCE, New American Library
1633 Broadway, New York, New York 10019